HOLOGRAM

HOLOGRAM

A NOVEL

PADGETT POWELL

OPEN ROAD

INTEGRATED MEDIA

NEW YORK

Cover design by Jason Gabbert

978-1-4804-6417-9

This edition published in 2014 by Open Road Integrated Media, Inc.
345 Hudson Street
New York, NY 10014
www.openroadmedia.com

FOR NAN MORRISON

HOLOGRAM

"After all, I think Forrest was the most remarkable man our Civil War produced."

—General William Tecumseh Sherman

"Forrest, . . . had he had the advantages of a thorough military education and training, would have been the great central figure of the Civil War."

—General Joseph E. Johnston

"General N. B. Forrest of Tennessee, whom I have never met, . . . accomplished more with fewer troops than any other officer on either side."

—General Robert E. Lee

HOLLINGSWORTH

———◄○►———

Mrs. HOLLINGSWORTH LIKES TO TRAIPSE. Her primary worry is thinning pubic hair, though this has not happened yet. She is bothered that a thought of this sort could occur to her at all, let alone with some frequency. She enjoys a solidarity with fruit. She is wistful for the era in which hatboxes proliferated, though a hatbox is not something even her grandmother may have owned. More probably what she wants is hatboxes themselves, without the era or the hats. But the proud, firm utility of the hatbox requires a hat and an era for its dignity; otherwise it is a relic. She does not want relics. Her husband is indistinct. She regards friendly dogs with suspicion. Her daughters have lost touch with her, or she with them, or both; it is the same thing, she thinks, or it is not the same thing, which means it might as well be the same thing: so much is pointless this way, indifferent, moot, or mute, as a friend of hers says. Not a friend, but a friendly man whom she cannot bring herself to correct when he says "mute" for "moot," for then she might have to go on and indict his entire presumption to teach at the community college, inspiring roomfuls of college hopefuls to say "mute" for "moot" and filling them with other malaprops, and if she indicts him on that presumption she'll need to go on and indict him for the presumption of his smug liberalism and for affecting to like film as Art and not movies as entertainment and for getting his political grooming from the smug liberalism and film-as-Art throat clearing of National Public Radio, and all of this, since it would be but the first strike in taking on the entire army of modest Americans who believe themselves superior to other Americans (but not to any foreigners, except dictators) mostly by virtue of doing nothing but electing to think themselves superior—all of this would be unwise, or moot, and indeed she may as well be mute, maybe the oaf was on to something.

She wanted to summon a plumber and pour something caustic down the crack of his ass when he exposed it to her, as he invariably would when assuming the plumbing position. Drano, she thought, très apropos. She had learned recently that the British term for the propensity of the working man to expose himself in this way was "showing contractor's bottom." That was a lovely touch of noblesse oblige, of gently receding empire.

She was less gentle in her apprehension that the entire world and everyone in it was showing its ass. She was not unaware, and not happy, that this apprehension linked her closely to the film-as-Art side of the herd, and she would go to a movie with a plumber wearing no pants at all before she'd go to some *noir* with a man

6

in slacks, but still she found herself actually calculating the drift of things if one were to try to burn a contractor's bottom. She figured on this seriously all one morning until finally she faced it: it had come to this, had it? Her mind had gone. The practical consequences of her symbolically telling the world to pull its goddamn pants up filled up her otherwise empty head at age fifty. It had all come to this. Muriatic acid for the driveway contractor, liquid chlorine for the pool man, shot of Raid for the bug man, upgrade the plumber to a bead of molten solder. When this nonsense left her mind alone, she thought about the Civil War. How a woman could be prevented from doing anything but thinking of contractor's bottom, and of all which that represented, and of all her impotence at reversing the disposition of the human world to show its ass, was owing somehow to the Civil War. The American Civil War, arguably as silly a war as they come, she was virtually ignorant of. She was not better informed of any war, actually, save for perhaps the Second World War and Vietnam, on a very topical basis. And she knew of one man who had been in Korea. But the Civil War . . . was beginning to haunt her.

She could not reckon this sudden absorption with it, given how vastly uninformed she was of it. Manassas was molasses, Sharpsburg was Dullsville; the March to the Sea was no more than Hard to Lee. Her images of the dead, which she did know to nearly exceed the dead of all our other wars combined, were not those of the bodies themselves that the wet-plate photography so in its infancy had allegedly recorded in such stunning graphic detail. She kept seeing not bodies but crows on them. To her, true torment was not death but a crow.

The thousands of baleful tears shed then now went, she thought, into laundry softener—the women threw these handkerchiefs of the laundromat into their machines as they had thrown kerchiefs at military parades. The result was every bit as good: things smelled sweet and the women felt good about themselves. Their men marched on in the perfume of goodfeeling and put their cell phones to their heads and zeroed in on the enemy and fired nonsense at him all day. They had learned from Vietnam how to drop smoke on the enemy to target him better. There was much information. It was not clear when everyone had stopped believing in himself.

A prison term was not the worst thing that could obtain in this age, she thought. Nothing was. Nothing was the end of the world. All could be surmised and survived. Death and rape were just particularly bad. We were mature. But crows could land, after all; they need not fly all day long. And you had to regard them.

She knew that the Confederate mint in Columbia had printed its worthless millions and stood today in vacant ruin, but virtually intact, for sale at too high a price to sell to whoever would turn it into a museum or a mall. She knew that Appomattox is a National Park, fully restored, visited by thousands of tourists a year. She knew that only 4 percent of the final site of the Lost Cause is original, based on the number of original bricks compared to the total number of unoriginal bricks used in the restoration. She knew that this restoration had had to commence from the very archaeological digs that had discovered the outlines of the foundation of the house where it all ended. None of the bricks was even in its original location. Only some stones of the hearth are in the same place. Beyond that, only the *airspace* is the original thing, where it was. Maybe a piece of furniture or two that Grant and Lee might have *looked* at. And she knew about Lee's ingenious battle orders that the Yankees found wrapped around dropped cigars. That business amazed and frightened her. And the name Nathan Bedford Forrest was in her head like the hook of a pop-radio tune. In her grasp of it all, he was a man who had somehow never been beaten in a war that was lost from the start. She knew more than she knew she knew.

On her kitchen table she noticed an odd, tall can of Ronson's lighter fluid. There had not been a cigarette lighter of the sort that required this fuel in this house in she would guess twenty years. It would squirt down a contractor's bottom as pretty as you please. She chuckled. She was not herself, she thought, or she was, perhaps, and she chuckled again.

Were men who could not keep their pants up a function of the Civil War? Were women who put up with them a function of the Civil War? Was having yourself an indistinct husband a function of the Civil War? Was finding a strange bottle of flammable petroleum distillate beside your grocery list a function of the Civil War? Was chuckling and not knowing what was yourself and what was not yourself a function of the Civil War? Was not really caring at this point "who you were," and finding the phrase itself a hint risible, a function of the Civil War? She sat down at the table and wrote on her grocery list, "A mule runs through Durham, on fire," and then, dissatisfied with merely that, sat down to augment the list.

CORNPONE

———◄○►———

Mrs. HOLLINGSWORTH WROTE ON:

A mule runs through Durham, on fire. No—there is something on his back, on fire. Memaw gives chase, with a broom, with which she attempts to whap out the fire on the mule. The mule keeps running. The fire appears to be fueled by paper of some sort, in a saddlebag or satchel tied on the mule. There is of course a measure of presumption in crediting Memaw with trying to put out the fire; it is difficult for the innocent witness to know that she is not just beating the mule, or hoping to, and that the mule happens to be on fire, and that that does not affect Memaw one way or another. But we have it on private authority, our own, that Memaw is attempting to save the paper, not gratuitously beating the mule, or even punitively beating the mule. Memaw is not a mule beater.

The paper is Memaw's money, perhaps (our private authority accedes that this is likely), which money Pawpaw has strapped onto his getaway mount, perhaps (our private authority credits him with strapping the satchel on, but hesitates to characterize his sitting the mule as he does as a deliberate, intelligent attempt to actually "get away"); that is to say, we are a little out on a limb when we call the mule, as we brazenly do, the mount on which he hoped to get away, and might have, had he not, as he sat on the plodding mule, carelessly dumped the lit contents of the bowl of his corncob pipe over his shoulder into the satchel on the mule's back, thereby setting the fire and setting the mule into a motion more vigorous than a plod. A mule in a motion more vigorous than a plod with a fire on its back attracts more attention than etc.

Memaw, we have it on private authority, solid, was initially, with her broom, after Pawpaw himself, before he set fire to the satchel behind him, so the argument that Pawpaw might have effected a clean getaway without the attention-getting extras of a trotting mule on fire is somewhat compromised. Memaw, with her broom, has merely changed course; she wants, now, to prevent her money's burning more than Pawpaw's leaving, though should Pawpaw get away with the money unburnt, she presumably loses it all the same. That loss, of unburnt money, might prove temporary: unburnt money is recoverable sometimes, if the thieves are not vigilant of their spoils, if the police are vigilant of their responsibilities, if good citizens who find money are honest and return it, etc. But burnt money is not recoverable, except in certain technical cases involving banks and demonstrable currency destruction and mint regulations allowing issue of new currency to replace the old, which cases Memaw would be surprised to hear about. And it is arguable that were she indeed whapping Pawpaw and not the fire behind him, her object might be not to prevent his leaving but to accelerate it.

So Memaw is now whapping not the immediate person of Pawpaw but the fire behind him. It is not to be determined whether Pawpaw fully apprehends the situation. He may think Memaw's consistent failure to strike *him* with the broom is a function of her undexterous skill with the broom used in this uncustomary manner. We are unable, even with the considerable intelligence available from our private authority, to hazard whether he knows the area to his immediate rear is in flames. Why Memaw would prefer to extinguish the fire rather than annul his escape or punish him for it is almost certainly beyond the zone of his ken. We have this on solid private authority, our own, our own *army* of private authority, in which we hold considerable rank. Pawpaw is maintaining his seat, careful to keep his clean corncob pipe from the reach of Memaw's broom, errant or not. Were the pipe to be knocked from his hand, either by a clean swipe that lofts it into the woods or by a glancing blow that puts it in the dirt at the mule's hustling feet, he would dismount to retrieve it and thereby quit his escape. It is likely that Memaw and the burning mule would continue their fiery voyage, leaving him there inspecting his pipe for damage.

The mule is an intellectual among mules, and probably among the people around him, but we, the people around him, intellectuals among people or not, as per our test scores, our universities and degrees therefrom, and our disposition to observe public broadcasting, and with the entire army of private authority we command, cannot know what he knows. It is improbable that he knows of Pawpaw's betrayal, of Memaw's hurt rage, of the accidental nature of the fire, of the denominations of the currency, of the improbable chance that among the money are dear letters to Memaw before she was Memaw that she does not want Pawpaw to discover, even after he has left her and might be presumed to be no longer jealous of her romantic affairs. It is not certain that he, the mule, knows his back, or something altogether too close to his back, is on fire. It is certain, beyond articulated speculation, that he senses his back is hot and that the kind of noise and the kinds of colors that make him hot and nervous when he is too near them are on his back. He has elected to flee, or is compelled to flee. Nervousness puts him in a predisposition to flee. A woman with a broom, a two-legger with any sort of prominent waving appendage, coming at him puts him in full disposition to flee, which he does, which increases the unnerving noises and colors and heat on his back, confirming him in the rectitude of this course of action, notwithstanding certain arguments that he has almost certainly never heard and might or might not comprehend were he to hear them that he'd be better off standing still.

That is Memaw's position: if the bastard would just stand still, she could save him *and* the money. She could get Lonnie Sipple's letters out of the money, get the money out of the bag, then get Pawpaw, as he stupidly yet sits the mule guarding his pipe, which she could verily whap into the woods with one shot, and then get Pawpaw and the mule on down the road, where they are fool enough to think they want to go. She knows the mule is not fool enough to want to go down the road—the mule would appear to be a faultless fellow until caught up in human malfeasance and crossfire and dithered by it; plus he is on fire—but she is going to uncharitably link him to Pawpaw during the inexact thinking that prevails during domestic opera of this sort. This is precisely the kind of inexact thinking in which it does not occur to one that burnt money can be replaced at a bank under certain technical circumstances which make one nervous to speculate upon in the event that the money concerned is one's own. But now that the army of our private authority has revealed the further intelligence of the existence of personal letters, also in the satchel, we know that the money was never Memaw's first concern in her zealous whapping of the fire on the mule. And we know that Memaw, no matter how inexact her thinking during domestic opera of this sort, is not inclined to think that letters, like money, can be replaced, under certain technical circumstances, after they are burnt. Letters of the sort she is protecting now, in fact, are themselves but the thinnest substitute for, papery vestiges of, the irreplaceable tender emotions they recall, tender emotions that she held and that held her in a state of rapt euphoria some thirty years ago, emotions she can but vaguely recollect when she holds the letters in her rare few moments of calm, tired tranquillity. She and Lonnie Sipple are only nineteen years old, they kiss without the nuisances of whiskey and whiskers and malodorous thrusting, without the complications of bearing children, and Lonnie Sipple has not yet been found with the pitchfork tine through his heart.

Pawpaw is, in contrast to Lonnie Sipple in this recollected tender tranquillity, and in the loud, mean, prevailing domestic opera that surrounds her small tranquillities like a flood tide, a piece of shit what thinks it won World War II and thereby earned the right to be every kind of shitass it is possible to be on earth, and then some, if there is any then some. This, his single-handed winning of WWII, is inextricably and inexplicably a function of his people's collective losing of the Civil War eighty years before.

Memaw did not become Memaw until she allowed herself to be linked to Pawpaw via a civil ceremony during the post-war frenzy of imprudent coupling that wrought more harm to the country, she now thinks, than Hirohito. She had a normal name and was normal herself. She was Sally, and a fond uncle had called her Salamander, which now, against Memaw, sounds charming. And Pawpaw had been Henry Stiles until two minutes after the ceremony, when people seemed to come out of the woods and the woodwork all calling him Pawpaw and her nothing, ignoring her for a full two years, it seems, until slowly addressing her, tentatively at first but then unerringly, as Memaw. She was powerless to stop this phenomenon; it was not unlike a slow, rising tide, unnoticed until it is too late to escape. There she had been, first on a wide isolated silent mudflat of wedding-gift Tupperware and their VFW mortgage, and then in a sudden full sea of *Memaw* and only a thin horizon of sky and water around her. It stunned her to hear "Memaw makes the best cornpone," stunned her into hearing it again and again, and then Sally was never heard of or from, and she was not a Salamander but a Hellbender.

We have it from the army of private authority that dogs

love Memaw. Two dogs are, in fact, at her heels as she herself dogs the heels of the mule, of which dogging she is tiring, and Pawpaw, who dropped his pipe and voluntarily quit the mule to retrieve it, having grown complacent with his surmise that his pipe is unhurt, is in an awkward amalgam of embarrassment and fatigue and uncertainty as to what to do now. Memaw is between him and his burning getaway mule, and he is more winded than Memaw and the mule, so that the matter of his skirting around Memaw and overtaking the mule himself is out of the question. He is somewhat concerned—even the innocent witness can deduce this, by the nervous motions of his feet when she turns occasionally to glare at him and point one long finger at him—that Memaw will desist pursuit of the burning mule and come after him, which will put him in the face-losing position of having to retreat.

Keeping his distance, as he is, he has had occasion to pick up pieces of charred currency and an envelope with a canceled stamp on it dated 1943, which he knows was the war because he knows (first to bloom in his troubled brain at this moment, this is to say) of the 1943 steel penny, a copper-conservation thing owing to the war, which he knows (second to bloom) he was in, which he knows (third) because he won it. The letter is addressed to Sally Palmer in a handwriting not his own.

This was the best grocery list Mrs. Hollingsworth had ever conceived. There were things on it that obviously suggested you need not go to the store only to be disappointed over not getting them. She sat at her table marveling at the fun of such a grocery list. She was going to make a few of these. Yessireebob, she said to herself, slapping at a fly. This was a bit more like it. She studied for a moment her linoleum floor, which had a nice old agate speckle to it and made a sound like something breaking when you walked on it.

BLUEGILL

———◇———

Mrs. HOLLINGSWORTH HAD READ or heard some things about Nathan Bedford Forrest. She had to have. It was the name of the high school. Had she read of him as well? The idea had formed in her mind that he had been indomitable; he had been the War's Achilles. Achilles with pinworms and slaves besmirching his heroic profile. Had she heard even that the South could have won had he been given broader command? He seemed listable.

She put him on:

A man who has seen Forrest catches two bluegills at one time on his hook, on his cane pole, noticing as he does, inexplicably, an exotic fish—parrotfish? yellowtail?—in the water. The fish is as odd as his vision of the Civil War figure: a strange waking dream of a man on a horse larger and louder than Hollywood, whom he somehow knew to be representing Nathan Bedford

Forrest. In the same spirit of unblinking improbability he saw what looked like a pompano in the dark lake, now the two blue-gills. He enters the dockhouse to show the improbable catch to his wife. In the dim shack he sees a leg in tight polyester shorts hanging awkwardly off a cot, and as the party wakes up he realizes the leg is not his wife's. "Excuse me, sir—ma'am," he says to a fogged woman who looks like his father's sister a bit, but more bleached. He intends to explain everything, including how and why a man up to something, as it appears a man this close to a strange woman sleeping must be, would not loom over her like this with two fish on a pole. Only an honest bumbler would do that. Why this woman is where his wife should be, and in a drunken stupor, he cannot begin to decide. He says to her, holding forth the two fish as she begins to focus on him for an explanation of his intrusion, "The escapees of the hattism of dived-in-ness." By "hattism of dived-in-ness" he seems to mean regularity of conformity.

The man was named Lonnie Sipple before he forgot who he was because of his broken heart.

FORREST

—Do you see our leader with his hair on fire riding like—

—No.

—the wind?

—I didn't even see that he was on a horse.

—You'd better get with it, then. If your leader rides by with his hair on fire slapping at you with the flat of his saber so as to inspire you or goad you or outright scare you to heroics beyond yourself, and taking up falterers by the collar and throwing them to constitute roadblocks before other falterers, and otherwise threatening them with sufficient otherworldly gesture that they become convinced simple mortality is less dreadful than what he promises them if they run, and so they decide to turn and fight, and thank him later, whether they are dead or alive—if you do not see this going on about you, you are in trouble.

—I did not see "my leader." I am not aware that I am being led. Or that I follow.

—Then you are in deep, deep trouble, my friend. I should take this can of Ronson here—who bought this? for what? very pretty can—and set *your* hair on fire.

—Maybe you should.

—This can reminds me of a bad high school football uniform, the loud blue-and-yellow combo. Hard to win in that rig.

—Red-and-black beats that every time.

—There's Forrest again!

—Where?

—*Right there!*

—I can't see him.

—It is true, then. Some people see him, and some do not.

—I'd just as soon not.

—Frankly, I do not know that you are wrong. Because I do not know what to do with myself when I have seen him ride through a town square, horse and hair aflame, salt and leather and sweat and steel penetrating the trailing air, and a malaise of sadness and loss consuming all witness to him, leaving us diffident and afraid and idle in his wake.

—Maybe you should shoot him.

—The bullet would tink off him like a piece of errant solder. It would lie molten and deformed, splashed in the dirt. One side of it would shine and the other would be dulled by annealed dirt. It would be a symbol. Of something.

—Indeed. But what?

—I would not know. I failed Symbol.

22

—I failed Meta-everything.

—High five to that! But still, I can see Forrest, and you cannot.

—You have not failed Forrest.

—No, I have not. I will not fail Forrest. Forrest was made so that a man, even a confused one, a little afraid, or a lot, might not fail him, and thereby might not fail himself.

—He sounds like Jesus, sort of. But I failed Jesus too.

—Let's not get into that. This is enough: a man whose head and horse are on fire storms through town squares under my minute inspection. He is either there, invisible to the townsfolk his passing would otherwise knock down or blow down, or only there in my perhaps specially tuned vision. To me it does not matter how he exists, or why. I see him, he leads, I follow. Sometimes that means I go into the closest café on the square and have coffee. But I do what I can do. Even the terms of society are clear in a café after Forrest passes. The waitress in white or light green is tired but polite. The drunk is at the counter. The regulars are at their table, sclerotic and suspendered, gouty and flushed and content. And I am I, on my Mars, dithered even by the choices on a country breakfast menu, so all I have is coffee. But I have seen Forrest. I am not doing badly.

ROOM

THE MAN WHO HAS SEEN FORREST takes a room over the café. How long he will want the room he does not know. It is white. The floor is oak, with a gymnasium certainty to it, clean and hard. He wants nothing on it. He has one chair, by the window. There is a radio. It is black and on, but silent. A red stereo-indicator light shows, and a comforting green luminescent tuning band. The man is unsure whether he has found this appliance (improbable) or brought it (improbable). The tuning band shows the same comforting green light that originally issued from radium in such an application. He considers, not seriously, throwing the radio out the window.

Out the window, on the courthouse lawn, wearing blazing white shirts and loose herringbone trousers held up by handsome suspenders, are three or four or five or six or seven black men who appear to be ancient. Realistically—a word or notion that rolls saltily and oddly in the man's head, like an olive—they are probably seventy years old, but the impression they give is that they were alive when the great minié-ball debate over their fate took place. Like the radio, they too are on and silent and improbably placed. What they are discussing the man has no idea, in their immaculate clothes, consummately sober and peaceful and wise-looking, immutable agreeable whiskate.

The man turns and looks at his four plain walls and regards them as an invitation to rest.

Down on the courthouse lawn, he makes four plain mistakes.

—Gentlemen (#1), what town is this? I mean (#2), I've been driving and enjoying the scenery (#3), and my map is torn right where I think this is, I can't read where I am, I think.

—Where your map?

—In my car.

—Where your car?

The man waves vaguely behind himself (#4). He looks up at the window of his new room. He sees himself smiling and smirking at his intelligence-gathering mission among the seated sages.

—Holly Spring.

—Holly Spring what?

—Holly Spring *what* what?

—Which Holly Spring?

—*This* Holly Spring.

—Which *state* Holly Spring?

—*State?*

—He say his map bad.

—His map *real* bad.

—Missippi.

—Mississippi?

—Missippi.

The man waves to himself in his window, not concealing his waving to no one from the dark sages, which is not mistake #5. It says to them, Lost? Maybe loster than you think, gentlemen.

He claims his room for his rest.

The bed is as loose in its springs as a hammock. The sheet is a coarse, clean muslin that is very agreeable, as is his near engulfment into the slung posture of the mattress. He hears a noise, probably under the floor, probably a rat.

What he would like it to be is a woman. He thinks: tunneling her way to me. Let her emerge from this clean, hard floor, splintering it with her desire for me, and let me bathe her and place her on a pallet on the floor and behold her. Let us eat. Let us have each other in a fresh way in a fresh start and keep it fresh, keep it starting. To have a woman in perpetual start!

WOMAN

———◦———

EMERGING FROM THE FLOOR, she is gauzy, dark, as if seen through frosted glass, full red lips prominent. At this moment, before the ruination can begin, the man is happy. He has been a Gila monster and is now a puppy. The woman has strong hands and does not fidget with them. This, the man says, let us keep it to this. His lips are numb.

—Wait until you get a load of Forrest.

The woman posts herself on the chair by the window, and the man watches her watch for Forrest. Her red lips are blued with the pressure of her determination.

—Were you Lonnie?

—Were you Sally?

—Shh.

MOTHER OF FATHER,
FLAT OF KNIFE

————◄○►————

Fist, skull, stomp, gouge, *RIDE!* Forrest says, when you are the fastest with the mostest until you are the leastest with the lastest. (Mrs. Hollingsworth thought Forrest actually said some of this.) He is through the gentlemen of ebony tribal regalness and elegant white shirts in an unseen unfelt blast of oilcloth and horse lather and unsmelt tang of silver spur, the flat of his saber in abeyance.

The man who can see him recalls that the mother of his father would slap his father with the flat of her carving knife. She was a great proud carver, which women seldom are, of ham and tongue, and she did not like pickers picking at her work. Her knife was red-handled and pitted, a blackened steel that showed a shiny edge. She slapped the hands of children regularly with it. She could tell a child a lie.

Forrest is a ghostly trail of dust and sweat and malice, a struck chord of straining tack and sheathed weapon and purpose. His lips are set in a line not unlike the new woman's, but they do not show the blue of the pressure of determination, as hers do. Forrest's lips are easy, deliberate without deliberation, exactly like a horse's lips. He is an animal, all right, the man says. Did you see him?

—I saw him. I thought him wizened. I read that he declined.

—Declined what?

— No, *declined*. Fell off some. Withered. At the end.

—If he declined, Lord let him not incline.

—No.

FIRST BREAST NOT
OF ONE'S MOTHER

———◄○►———

WHEN HIS GRANDMOTHER, who could tell a child a lie,
with pleasure, pursing her lips after it in a satisfied way, as if
savoring a chocolate, died, Lonnie Sipple cried. The look on his
grandmother's face when she told him a lie was the same as the
look on her face when she played poker.

When he met Sally Palmer and with his lips lifted her
breast by a gentle pursing of the flesh just below her nipple,
and felt the orangelike weight of her breast, it was the last
clear moment of sanity and purpose on earth he would know.
It was possibly the first such moment, but he cannot remember anything before the moment, and cannot precisely recall
the moment itself, and all since has been a sloppiness in his
head and his heart.

He did not die of a pitchfork tine to the heart. That was
romantic palaver of the burning-mule stripe, and far too easy.

He did in fact once *find* a tine, isolated and alone, in a field, but it did not touch his heart. It had about it a roughened, pitted quality not unlike his grandmother's carving knife. All steel, he thinks, was more or less alike in those days.

RIDE, SLIDE

—◁o▷—

"Most times Forrest rides," Mrs. Hollingsworth began her list one day, thinking of the way the teenagers in the neighborhood talk and slink around, or slump around, being wiggers. Most time Mist Forrest ride but sometime he slide.

Sometime he take off his butternut duster look like Peterman catalogue, and his Victoria Secret garter belt and all, and grease hisself up naked as a jaybird and say, Okay, I fight all you, black white blue gray I don't care. Y'all come on. And people being dumb as shit, they come on, and they get they ass *whup.*

He so good he go to a wrassling tournament in Turkey once, during a time when he spose be recovering from a ball to the hip, which is how you say he got shot in them days. Never heard that about no Vietnam: my buddy he took dis ball to the hip, but he rode on! Shit. Em all saying, Found my buddy wid his balls in his mouf! Everybody drunk and all, going to the VA get pills. But back in Forrest time, it was ball to the hip, like soccer, and you went on, and went back later and kilt mo Yankee. One time I say to this honky on his bicycle, Clean up America, kill a redneck today! and it kind of surprise him. I guess since I *look* white and all. I'own know why he surprise, actually. Near everything surprise the white boy, that why he so *white*. He sur*prise* all the time.

But Forrest he go to Turkey one time on hip-ball furlough and get in a wrassling tournament to hep speed his recovery and he line up and grap holt em boys all grease up and naked and he a *natural*. He just as good as them what done this all they life, and then they see it gerng be more to it than that. He git worked up and start slobbering on they ass. He slobber so much he win; they think he sick or got rabies or something. They start call him Deve, mean camel, he slobber so much like a camel slobber when it wrestle a camel. Deve win entire damn show. The Camel is very good, they say, Deve cok iyi. Then Forrest take his trophy and have a beer with them and come home and don't win the rest of the war cause Prez Davis homo for Genel Bragg, who don't like Forrest and won't give him no guns and shit. Which it is maybe good for us on skateboards and in these humongoid pants and all today, because Forrest they say hard on the nigga, so he ain't gone cut no wigga no slack either, and we be in it too if he'd a won, but I don't know if he so hard on the black man as all that, cause one time a man say to Forrest, Hey Genel, how come you so hard on the Negro?

I ain't hard on the Negro, Genel Forrest say. *Jesus* hard on the Negro, buddyro.

Mrs. Hollingsworth was pretty pleased with that, and she knew that no raphead dufus rebel on a skateboard could come up with it (and she wondered how she knew of Braxton Bragg's vendetta for Forrest), or sound like that if he did. It was *her* grocery list. She was no longer shopping for the mundane.

She sat her days at her kitchen table with a pot of something cooking slowly on the stove, a small blue flame and a small gurgle in the room with her. Anyone who saw her making this prodigious, preposterous list saw nothing awry. Her indistinct husband remained indistinct. She was beginning to enjoy a new kind of freedom, one that she hadn't suspected existed. She was shopping in heaven, and hell.

ETERNITY, EPIPHANY

Sᴀʟʟʏ ᴀɴᴅ Lᴏɴɴɪᴇ, after this weighing of her left orange by Lonnie's lips, locked up their eyebeams, intertwixt and gratifying, for about a tenth of a second, which is all people can stand when there is the real intertwixtment and which seems like, or more like, about a eternity, which is the time required, or about the time allotted, for a epiphany.

They would neither of them again enjoy the intertwixtment, the crackle of iris to iris, the hope of pupil pooling pupil. Fried marbles and deep holes of loneliness suddenly alive, and answered prayers they had not known they were praying—not again. They would fancy it again, of course; they would have to, or they would die of despair. But it would never happen, the true spoiling of the film of their hearts, again.

BLUES

—◄○►—

THE WOMAN SITS AT THE WINDOW, her vanilla flesh smart on the black-lacquered straight chair. Her breast catches an odd orange light glaring from the sill of the window. She sees Forrest blow through the square, his duster like a robe behind him, the jangle of tack and weapon like a badly reproduced music of some sort, or heard from far away. Like, she thinks, country blues played over a plywood floor, amplified in weird imbalance balancing well with the congruently weird acoustics of the cheap tired joint the music is played in, heard from outside in the swamp near the roadhouse. A thumping is prominent, not un-sexual, and a tinny kind of sweet but wounded melody plays over it, from strings that are stretched by callused fingers that picked cotton in ancestoryear—

—Do you always think elaborate hoohah like that? the man says.

—You can read my mind?

—I might as well. It'll save blather, don't you think?

—Don't look me in the eye like that. Look at my body. It is what I give you.

—I can accept that. Give it to me, then.

—Because if I was Sally, I am not now.

—Shh.

—We are skeletons with meat on them.

—You have godly meat.

—Thank you.

—Your godly meated skeleton can think Forrest a music heard in a swamp, though. A music that will not quit, or a thinking of it that can't quit, even when the skeleton and the meat have quit.

—Do you always think hoohah like that?

—Only under force of circumstances.

— Such as?

—These. Don't look me in the eye either.

LOVE, SELF

———◄○►———

IF MRS. HOLLINGSWORTH WERE to go to the store with this list, she was aware, it would not feed anyone in whatever combination she assembled the ingredients on it. There was not a satisfying meal to be made of it. There was in some rarefied sense a meal to the second or third power, perhaps what you could call a meal prime, which would satisfy only a hungry fool. That, she decided, was who, other than herself, she was shopping for. There was a hungry fool in the world with whom she had something in common, and maybe for whom she had something.

On her lawn outside were some boys cheering the O.J. Simpson verdict, skateboards aloft like swords.

She wrote herself a note, as one does sometimes on a shopping list, a kind of rider reminder to the main reminder that is the list itself:

Dear Love,

How have you come to be a black-hearted woman with your come-and-go eyes? You is a storm of bad ideas. You will never be allowed to speak on National Public Radio. You enjoyed Flaubert when you were a girl, that is true. How have you become Celine? I love you anyway.

Love,
Self

PREVARICATING & PROCRASTINATING, SHUCKIN & JIVIN

———◄○►———

—MAN DON'T KNOW WHAT *state* he in!

—Say his map bad.

—Worses map I ever hoid of.

—In *trouble* you don't know what *state* you in.

—I saw boy one time, cuhn put this six-pack beer in paper sack. I say, Boy, you fumble widda piece a pussy like you fumblin widdat sack, you in *trouble*!

—What he say?

—He ain say shit. Turn red as a baby, a crab moreso. Bout to cry right in that sto.

—You talks funny, Erasmus. Say "widdat" and "sto," and I bet you say "ho," what hell else you gone say, but even you is not gerng say "Ise gwyne down to duh ribber," or maybe, if the lady here will cooperate, you is. She ain know what she doin. She done put you and all us on her grocery list.

—I believe, Satch, that the departures in my diction from the true path are justified given the trail of travail our tongue has trippingly took to be at dis point. They is, as I know you know, and it bruise me to point this out to you, procrastinating and prevaricating on the one hand, which would be the white hand, since I am being so crystal clear this morning, and shuckin and jivin on the other hand, and we all know out here on the court-house lawn whose hand that is. Speaking of which, I feel a bad breeze blowing somewhere, do you?

—I smell a horse. I am askeert of a horse.

—Something like ammonia blow through here.

—What *state* he in!

—I been *loss,* but never like dat!

—Amenhotep to that.

—Who?

—Jesus, another name for Jesus.

—Is?

—Might as well be. Jesus *hard.*

—That he is. That he is for sho.

THE LAND

———◄◦►———

Forrest could never talk this way, so Mrs. Hollingsworth made him:

Dark now only when the station wagon headlights do not
illuminate it, rolling over its swell and slough, crushing what is
left of its game, the urban-adapting coon, the strange-no-matter-
where-you-put-him possum. The snakes are flattened to dust and
blown away into herpetological archives. The alligator and the
deer have received protection. All the rest have been allowed to
perish.

The trees are under cultivation, bristling like large weeds,
rent this way and that and spindly, after a not thorough job of
weeding by a hasty, mad hand getting out of the garden before
sunstroke sets in.

That is the land, the wilderness. The pristine tracts of the
new wilderness are the fresh expanses of asphalt around the

malls. A new petroleum air of virgin potential resides there, but only until the Volvos and the skateboards pull in. The Volvos discharge baby strollers and easy-listening FM, the skateboards the funk of boys, all taming the new wilderness.

QUEERS AND CIGARS

FORREST MIGHT TALK LIKE THIS, so she let him:

Hard on the Negro? *Jesus* is hard on the Negro, buddyro.
Negro hard on himself too. Still, I will tell you something. Given
Davis and Bragg over me, playing keep-away with the ordnance
and men, and Bobby Lee wrapping his battle orders around
cigars and giving them to the enemy, if the Negro were in charge
today we'd stand a sight better chance of winning this fight. The
Negro has not cost me one empty saddle at the end of a fight.
Them what talk for a living has. The Negro does not talk for a
living. Not yet.

CARP

———◄○►———

THE GOLDEN-FLOORED ROOM fills with golden carp. The oak is as hard and clean as marble slabs for fish in a proper *poissonerie.* The carp do not resist flooding into a rented room in Holly Springs Mississippi. The river has not been kind to them for some time. They relax. On the cot a man and a woman relax.

The carp say, "Psst!" and the woman props up on her elbow and beholds them. "Why, y'all are just a bunch of *lonely* boys," she says, affecting some kind of drawl that pleases the carp. The carp affect drawls themselves, among fishes, and they wonder how the woman knows to play with them like this, if she does know how and is not just goofing. The carp do not have time to speculate or to question the woman about this. Their time on the floor is limited, a fact they sense without knowing the limit.

"The floor is filled with fish, babe," the woman says to the man, who reclines on his back with his arm across his eyes.

"What kind?'

"Redhorse suckers."

"Hmm. Had me two bluegills at wunst on my onliest hook, saw a yellertail, din't see no carp." The man is doing put-on talk too. The carp are delighted with these people, their hosts.

The carp flow out of the room by the drain of the window, leaving the floor cleaner than it was before their tour. When they are back in the river, the river is kinder to them. All day they say, Wunst we went to a room, and the river says, Sure you did, boys.

BREAM BEDDING

———◦———

—I SMELL FISH. YOU smell fish?

—Smell like . . . no.

—Like bream beddin! That a smell now, people say you cain smell no fish under water but you sure as—

—We know that, Erasmus. Save it for the tourists.

—Ain no tourist.

—We know that too. What we do not know is why not. The Negro woman can hold a fond court among her handicrafts upon the roadside, or wrap her head and sell pancakes or God knows what else, baskets, you name it, and be blinded by flashbulbs. But I have yet to see a council of elders such as ourselves holding court on the courthouse lawn all the live-long day, as we do, with so much as one person interested in us at all.

—Cept if he don't know what *state* he in.

—Exception duly noted. Short of that, the white man has no use for us. Why is this?

—Is *we* got any use for us?

—Erasmus, that is entirely beside the point, existentially speaking.

—Well scuse the doowop out of me. I smell fish, an I tell you something: they come out that winder up there bout a half-hour ago, a funk parade to beat the band.

—You saw them—what, fish po out that window?

—Shet up wid yo po. No, Satchmo, they disnt not po out, I disnt not eben see em, I done smelt em, as I told you in a straight-forward reportorial manner innocent of shuck, jive, prevaricate, and procrastinate. If you were not so concerned with the want of a gaggle of tourists who you somehow fantasize could be inter-ested in us and the anachronistic reminder of the pox on their land that we represent, you would perhaps be in a position to *listen* to someone. When, ah mean, he speak to you. Bout some-thing impotent.

—Fish.

—Right on. Come out dat winder up yonder. Girl up in deah too, lookin *good.*

—With Mr. Whatstate?

—Yessiree. You tell me, existentially speaking, how a man don't know what state he in get a woman like that in his bed—you tell me that, existentially speaking, you be tellin me something.

DIFFERENTLY DIFFERENT

———◄◦►———

YOU COULD GET CIGARS and even guys at the grocery store, though not by fiat, Mrs. Hollingsworth reflected, but you could not get carp, or bluegill, or bream. She was getting stranger in her shopping wants. She was getting further from what was available. The meal she was assembling was going to satisfy only a hungrier, larger fool than the kind of fool she had originally thought she might invite to dinner.

This getting stranger did not bother her. It had been coming on for some time. She had felt restless, of course, in specific and vague ways, all her life, as have, she figured, all people paying sufficient attention to their lives to admit that their lives are utter mysteries. But lately there had been an agreeable yawning in her heart, a surmising of new hollow. She was trying to draw a breath of something with nothing visible or prudent in it, just *other* air. When she breathed this air, or tried to, or pretended to, or merely hoped to, she fancied that she was trying to breathe an air that no one near her cared or knew anything about. Her daughters, for example: they had makeup, men, ambition or not, they were fatigued or not, with the world or with her or not. Her husband was . . . well, himself. Men did not entertain the vapors, or if they did, which she allowed might happen, they went off the edge entire and wound up in institutions of either a gentle or a cruel kind. But there was a safe zone for women to lose their minds and remain among the zombies who had not, and to not be recognized as having lost their minds. The zombies, after all, were pretty slow to appreciate someone other than themselves, and they had been schooled not to denigrate the different. They were attending just now, in fact, a large adult-education academy, studying a curriculum that insisted there was no such thing as difference at all. The harbinger for this had been, she supposed, handicapped-person legislation. It had come from somewhere, and it had received a great activating boost of philosophically underpinning energy from the American academy, which had invented political correctness, a new language, to shore up the shaky proposition that there were no differences among people. Mrs. Hollingsworth discovered this when she went to the local university to take a night course in Coleridge and found instead, in the scheduled room at the scheduled time, a course entitled "Theorizing Diaspora, Adjudicating Hybridity."

On the blackboard, on a paper handout, and on individual CRT screens in front of each seat in the room was a statement:

The primary requirements are a strong commitment to visually expressing support for all students within our community. By displaying the provided sign or button, a Friend can send a message of acceptance or encouragement.

We encourage proposals on the rhetorical intersections of gender with race, class, age, sexuality, and ability; interpreting the academy, disciplinarity, and professional identities from a feminist perspective; reclaiming the lost or marginalized voices of women (e.g., rhetors, writers, teachers, artists, workers); analyzing the rhetoric of historical depictions of women; the rhetoric of the feminist movement and the feminist backlash; males and men's studies and scholarship in relation to feminism; extrapolations of theory from the everyday (e.g., etiquette manuals, cookbooks, diaries) . . .

Mrs. Hollingsworth was dazed by this, but snapped to at "cookbooks": was she perhaps, she wondered, already extrapolating theory from a grocery list? Maybe she had already written her paper for the course, if she could induce the professor to include grocery lists in the catalogue of extrapolatable genres. That odd phrase rolled in her brain a moment until she became aware that there was a man in sandals and socks speaking very softly and very self-assuredly at the head of the long table that they—she and some much younger students—were sitting at.

He was saying, ". . . the interactions of discourse and ideology—that is, how the work of the poet operates within a variety of prevalent romantic cultural discourses—e.g., romantic, amatory, religious, hedonist, colonialist—in order to collaborate with, challenge, oppose, or, in rare cases, subvert them." Here, at "subvert," the professor raised his eyebrows several times until everyone at the table chuckled, which it seemed to Mrs. Hollingsworth was the actual requirement so far of the course. She had failed to chuckle. At the same moment that she perceived everyone in the room to be staring at her very politely, she noticed in her hand a button of the pin-on political variety that said on it FRIEND.

Into the silence that apparently awaited something from her, Mrs. Hollingsworth said, "Are we going to read 'The Rime of the Ancient Mariner'?"

"You mean theorize diaspora, adjudicate hybridity?" the professor asked, with more of the eyebrow hydraulics.

She could not respond, so the professor, whose role seemed to be that of helping out the obtuse, went on: "We will focus on the ways in which diasporan subjectivity complicates and problematizes the relationship between theory and identity, on the one hand, and representation and collectivity, on the other."

This remark had the effect of liberating the other students from staring politely at her. When they resumed their fond gaze at the professor, Mrs. Hollingsworth left the room. In her one hand was the FRIEND button, in her other hand her purse. She had a headache and was breathing hard.

Now she understood a few things: that the American academy, which one might have thought the place to defend freedom of speech, had been the seat and soul of abrogating freedom of speech, if the first assault on its freedom can be said to be restricting, or handcuffing, speech. "Handicapped" had become there "physically challenged" and, ultimately, "differently abled." A student body of mixed race had become one that was diverse. The diverse engendered something around it called pluralism. Pluralism was the high good, a kind of manna that was supposed to feed the bees and nourish them into new heavenly forms that would not sting each other. Pluralism was going to stop race riots. Saying "the N word" was going to make the black man happy. We could still say "redneck," she had noticed. The day she heard it on NPR, she turned NPR off, not because broadcasters were still using the term, but because she knew one day they would not be. In fact, she had a vision of the quiet moment backstage at a Boston studio when a good, surprised correspondent was let go for saying "redneck" the last time it would be said.

Her getting stranger had something to do with this truly getting stranger the nation was about. She wanted to be somewhere else, so she was making her list.

FORREST AND BOBBY LEE

—BOBBY LEE, LET ME AST YOU, friend, what you boys upair in the high cotton wrapping up cigars in you battle orders and droppin em behind enemy lines for? I find fightin hard enough without that.

—That? That warnt but a thang.

—Warn't but a thang? Put some boy bones in the ground, dint it?

—Yeah. Yeah it did.

—Well then it warn't just no thang, Bobby E. Lee. I got out-right queers on my back down here and it cost me boy bones all day long and it ain't just a thang. We ain't got no cigars down here. And it ain't just a thang down here.

—You do go on, Genel.

—Do I, Genel? Where boy bones is concerned, I don't hold with the luxury of cigars.

—I take your point, Genel. I take your point.

—You keep on takin it, Genel.

Mrs. Hollingsworth wondered if this item were not too obscure for even a hungry fool to understand. That is probably because it is real, she thought. Few people could credit that the War might have been over had not battle orders from Lee been found wrapped around cigars and given to McClellan in time to avert Lee's annihilation of him in the Valley campaign. That was harder to believe, she thought, than that, say, Ted Turner might try to produce a species of media baby and fight the War again. She was having these vague visions of television technology and Forrest and a new soldier, a New Southerner. All of this, she thought, more probable than battle orders wrapping up cigars in enemy territory, a sad and ineluctable fact of history. She liked the day that allowed you to say "ineluctable," and also "eponymous."

FUNERAL

———◄○►———

THE MAN WHO COULD SEE FORREST and who would see
a yellowtail in a lake and who had known love when he was
Lonnie and saw Sally, and who had not known it later, went to
the funerals, one hard upon another, of his mother and his father.
Both of them were held in desertlike heat.

At the funeral of his father, to which he was late, he had to
have them open the coffin at the cemetery so he could see him.
He had never seen a dead man before. He said to his father, "Hey,
bud," a thing his father had said to him, which he had never himself said. He held his hand. He kissed him on the cold meat of his
forehead. No one at the cemetery saw this. In the heat they were
now concentrating on trying to leave. Deer flies and sportcoats
and good cars and some women who had liked his handsome
father were by the cars, ready to leave. He could have joined his
father in the expensive box that was designed to turn his father

into slime and for which he felt most sorry for his father, and they would not have seen this either.

At the funeral of his mother, he was not late, and he did not have to have the coffin opened because it had not yet been closed. He said, "Hey, Mom." He did not touch her. If he did, he cannot remember, but he can remember thinking he was probably not going to want to, and he does not remember any change of emotion when he saw her, so his memory that he did not touch her is probably correct.

Inside the funeral home at his father's affair, where he discovered his father already removed to the cemetery, was a vulgar employee whom he should have assaulted but did not. The man said, "Y'all come back now, y'heah?" and got away with it.

He walked out into the heat then, and saw Forrest for the first time. Forrest slapped at a prickly pear cactus with the flat of his saber, and the man might have thought of his father's mother slapping his father with the flat of her carving knife, but he did not. It was too hot to think. He then saw Sally at the grave and did not remember her. She introduced herself, and he said, "Oh, yes. Of course."

GIZMO

—<o>—

THE WOMAN WITH TAUT VANILLA FLESH sits on the black chair and regards the courthouse lawn. I don't see them, she says.

—Who?

—The redhorse suckers.

—Why should you?

—They went out this window.

—Oh.

She watches the square. Something odd catches her eye in the shadows. She looks at the black men, who see her. She looks back to the odd thing, under a store awning.

—There are two men watching this window.

—The sages?

—No. These are criminals of some sort. White. Looking at us with a gizmo.

—What kind of gizmo?

—High-tech gizmo.

—I am not worried about no high-tech gizmo.

—Well, these are pretty low-tech-looking boys wielding the gizmo, if that makes any difference.

—Might. Just might.

SCIENTISTS

———◁◦▷———

—I CAINT QUITE TELL if she can see him or not, Hod. I know *he* can.

—Whyont you run Forrest now?

—Shit, Hod, em nappy pappys already actin spooked. I run him right through them last time, they so whooped by it one of em says he smellin bream beddin!

—Naw.

— Swear to God.

—Well, all right. We got what we want anyway. If she can see him too, that a extra. Mr. Turner gone be very pleased with his field hands, I'd say. The New Southerner to order! Man who caint remember who he is, one; caint forget who he supposed to be, two; can see Forrest and be spooked by it and have half a idea what the hell it is, three: that was our orders. And to boot, to judge from the looks a her, he aint queer—

—That's a miracle, way it going.

—Theys more wrong in the world than being queer, Rape.

—They is? Like what? You hidin something from me, Hod?

—No. It aint nothing but a thang. Now see can she really see him. Put him on Talk. I bleve we in position for a bonus, Rape, Mr. Turner find out we got him a mating *pair*. Don't run him through them old men no more. No telling what this does to people.

—Fuck people *up* when they see it, I'd say.

—Yeah, but I mean when they don't.

—Make em smell bream when they don't. That much we know.

—Yeah, Rape. We a couple reglar scientists.

DANDY

THE WOMAN WHO NO LONGER IS SALLY, if she ever was, pays oblique attention to the two men under the awning who are pointing something around the square. Those are as solid a pair of ne'er-do-wells ever scuffed shoes, she says to the man.

—I'm tired.

—I'm tired too, love. But it's Ted Bundy and Lee Harvey Oswald down there aiming a ray gun at this window or I'm a coot on duck day.

And then she sees Forrest—of this, from her expression, there is no doubt in the minds of those who witness her seeing him.

Forrest appears unmounted, natty in shirt garters and whip-cord trousers, not his riding attire, and wearing silver spurs. He takes a position near a granite pedestal bearing a likeness of himself. He disregards it. He says, in a voice surprisingly high and piercing, "I jingle when I walk in these things. They become me, if I am a dandy, and I become a dandy when I walk. That is why I ride fist skull stomp gouge and resent the everliving shit out of appointed leaders who dick around with cigars and bury boys. The bones of boys, mark me, will mark us forever. I am fire."

Forrest turns to fire, his mouth a monalisa. His spurs melt into the ground like mercury.

God damn, the woman says.

OBSESSION

It OCCURRED TO MRS. HOLLINGSWORTH that she should do something with herself other than make this preposterous grocery list that was getting preposterouser with every item she added. It was taking on a powerful vigor of its own. The Bundy and Oswald figures, for example, had appeared on the list without her direct intention, it seemed. This equipment they had she could not properly identify except to know that it made holograms and was more technical than she was and appeared way more technical than this Bundy and Oswald who were charged with operating it. It was one thing to have a preposterous grocery list, she thought, and another to have a list you did not control.

So to do something other than the list she went out in the country for a drive and saw some cows and two white doves in a very green field. Then she went back home and organized the floor of her closet, matching shoes to boxes and noting that she had three expensive leather train bags and had not been on a train for twenty-five years. She did not in fact think a train bag was necessarily intended to go on a train. Then she sat back down at her kitchen table to resume the list. It was becoming obsessive, she told herself. She then told herself it was probably the absence, not the presence, of some good salubrious obsessions in a life that made it unsatisfying. What else did she have, really? In the end, a list like this one was better on the antibourgeois scale than one you actually went to the store with, wasn't it? That, going to the store, would result in tuna casserole and a marriage with *Joy of Cooking* in its background, which was precisely what she had and was precisely what had inspired her to sit down in this fugue about Forrest in the first place. So she listed on.

SPOT

———◄◦►———

ONLY BOY BACK AIR with Bobby Lee what could I hear fight ate lemons, believed in Jesus, and got hisself shot by his own men. And I am walkin round on spurs made from melted thimbles. We are in a spot.

The fair ladies of Memphis have done made me a pair of silver spurs and now caint sew. When they get what men back they gone get back from this fight, it aint gone matter. The woman is gone pay for this for the rest of her everliving life. She gone put up with shanks and heroes what wasn't there and the luckiest of fools what was. It aint gone make for no high cotton.

OPERATOR'S MANUAL

———◄○►———

—Reason she seen fish in the room, Rape, and em boys smelt em, and that dude saw a pompano in the lake, is you aint know how to run that thang. A yellertail in the lake! We lucky Forrest aint come over here and kilt us.

—Hod, excuse me, Hod, excuse me, but did you see a operator's manual? No, Hod, you did not. You did not see a operators manual with this ray gun, Hod. That woman is perfectly right in calling it that, because this is what it is. And ray guns just appear without no manuals, like in the movies, people just knowing how to run them. If you have a quarrel, take it up with Mr. Turner. I suppose he knows how to run it.

—If it's really his, he might. Maybe he found it.

—Christ Almighty, Hod, you are not rational. Mr. Turner does not *find* shit. He makes it or he buys it. The last thing he *found*

75

was himself in a position to make millions of dollars acause his daddy—

—Rape, he found *us,* didn't he?

—Point well taken. We don't count. What counts is him up there in that room, and we found him, and that does count.

—Read me them orders again.

—I caint.

—Why not?

—Lost em.

—Well, how we know we found what Turner wants, then?

—I committed the orders to memory, like General Longstreet.

—Remember them to me, then.

—I caint.

—Why not?

—I forgot what they said. Before you say anything stupid, let me inform you that *no,* committing something to memory is *not* the same thing as remembering what it said. Horse of a entirely nother color.

HAIR

———◦———

THE MAN HAS HIS ARM across his eyes because the glare from the floor, while comforting in its warm gold clarity and cleanness, is bright. He is tired. The woman has told him the room was full of fish, a matter he remembers now as one remembers sweet improbable lunatic moments from childhood when things did not depend on verisimilitude for their ratification. He is tired. He cannot remember not remembering Sally at the funeral of his father. He cannot remember that there is any connection between Sally and the woman in the room, or if he thought there was. He can remember only, and only sometimes, the citrusy heavy feel of her breast in his mouth, that last moment he fancied he knew who he was, well before he thought he knew who he really was, either then or now thinking of the way he must have thought then . . . he is tired. Sally? he says to the woman on the chair.

—I told you, shh.

The hair on his arm he can feel on his eyelids. It is a well-and manly-haired arm, and women have liked his hair and his arm, including the woman on the chair, of whom he can't remember why she reminds him of anyone at all, let alone Sally, and he doesn't think it was a good idea to put hair all over the human body like this. Nor should a man, or a woman, be slick like a hairless dog, but there should have been better thinking going into this rampant hirsuteness, in his tired view, with his hairy arm across his eyes against the nice hurtful glare.

FLOOD

———◄○►———

LOOKING AT THE BACK OF HIS EYELIDS, the man saw not the colors he had read were called phosgenes and that some famous artist had said looking at was all he wanted to do; he saw a fast vivid replay of scenes with his father. These were both scenes he had witnessed and those he had only heard about. Once his father slept under wet sheets in a bathtub in Yulee Florida it was so hot. His father punched a relative of the state's attorney general in the mouth at a country club in Tallahassee Florida once, and the attorney general, under whom his mother worked, and under whom she was afraid she would not work when it got out that her husband was punching his relatives at the country club, sent word by her to thank his father for punching the man. Once his father had his mother row them under a live oak while his father fished and they looked up and saw so many water moccasins that it scared not only his mother but his father too. His father said, "One or two, all right, but . . . ," and laughed. "He laughs *now*," his mother said.

His father told him of how his own father had not let him quit high school football after three weeks just because he was getting hurt. You finish what you start. So his father said he decided to hurt somebody back, and did not quit, and became locally famous once he reversed the hurt ratio. Yet when Lonnie Sipple went out for high school football, his father took him off the field and informed the coach he would not be back. His father had been in the Pacific but would not say anything about the war, except late in life to tell him how comically bad a soldier he had been, playing poker and drinking beer and being put on unscheduled picket duty and falling asleep in a bamboo tower. Once when Lonnie was in college his father visited him, and when he saw that his father was carrying a pistol for the road, he remarked that it looked paranoid, and his father was gone, home, when he came out of the bathroom. And then his father died, more or less. In a box that cost $5000 and looked like NASA could do something with it, and in fact had had to be cranked open with a stainless steel tool and sounded like a refrigerator opening when he had them open it in the desert, his father was turning to slime. His arm across his eyelids felt comparatively acceptable now. The room was filled with the golden light, and the woman was alive. He was too. But he was tired.

EGG

———◁◦▷———

Mrs. HOLLINGSWORTH REGARDED Hod Bundy and Rape
Oswald with misgivings beyond their unplanned presence on her
list. Was she herself a wigger in a dress in an idle kitchen? Was
she making fun of a history that should be hallowed? Was the
entire business of corrupting the memory of Forrest a charged
irreverence? This war that had come to haunt her: it was a colos-
sal waste and shame, and her Forrest put it mildly when he said
they were marked by the bones of boys. How could she make fun
of the bones of boys? She sat there. She put on an egg to boil and
sat there some more. How could she *not* make fun, she thought
finally, of the bones of boys? They might otherwise kill you.

She was in this regard malaligned for proper reverent living,
at least on bourgeois American earth, and she always had been.
She wondered if malaligned was the same thing as maligned. You
could not tell where elisions had obtained in English, unlike in

French. She recalled the first instance, perhaps, of her irreverent malalignment, and it was in French class. The teacher asked them to translate *le chat noir,* and she had popped out with "He shat black." The laughter was so immediate and forceful that she had had to go along with it and act as if she had fully intended this as a joke, and in fact it is true that in the middle of her answering she had seen that it was a joke, but in her impulse to speak the answer and to be first with the answer, she had not been aware of the egregious error that was coming with it. She in fact *still* wanted to read French articles as pronouns.

Her whole life, it seemed, had been this way: meaning no harm, she could say someone shat black. It got to be a force of habit, finally. She was the sort of person who did not say the cat is black if there was a chance, accidental or deliberate, not to. And it seemed a little late to put in for a character change. She was going to make her list for her meal for the largest fools starving on earth. "Come and get it, boys," she said aloud to the egg rumbling on the stove. "Call me Mama."

ORDERS

———◁○▷———

THE ONE CALLED HOD BUNDY said to the one called Rape Oswald, "Read me the orders again. I was too nervous to hear them good when Turner read them. Plus that Jane is a distraction."

Oswald put down his half of the equipment, which appeared to be a heavy power supply, connected by a large-gauge, multi-strand umbilical to the half of the equipment carried by Bundy, which looked like a camera or radar gun. Bundy was jerked to a halt by the tautening of this umbilical, because he had kept walking after Oswald deposited the power supply.

—God damn, Rape.

—God damn what, Hod?

—You might give a warning signal.

—You said stop.

—I said read me the orders. I didn't realize it was chewing gum and walking for you.

—The orders is tucked away.

—I see that now.

Oswald procured the orders in the form of a linty wad from his pants pocket. He procured two Swisher Sweet cigars from a box in his shirt pocket and handed one to Bundy and lit them both and read the orders aloud.

Locate a man who can recognize the hologram cast by this unit—which is charged out to your account and for which you are responsible—and moreover recognize the significance of the hologram (Bedford Forrest). My people in science tell me the emotionally disturbed man may prove most sensitive to this kind of image, but I do not want an unstable candidate. The successful candidate will serve as a prototype man for the New Southerner, a man, if I may say so, much like me, whom I will then have eugenically engineered to found a line of men in the New South who will perforce raise up the Old by eliminating the genetic dearth effected by the War, thereby eliminating contractor's bottom and other ills. Bring him to me.

Mrs. Hollingsworth thought it funny having Turner say "contractor's bottom." She was perfectly aware it was a "manipulation" of Turner, putting "her" words in "his" mouth, also a laughable idea at this juncture. Turner would say "plumber's ass," and Jane would stop him, Hanoi Jane would stop him. How a girl like that got a stud like Turner who could make money and sail a boat was beyond Mrs. Hollingsworth.

Bundy said to Oswald, "You get all that?"

Oswald said, "What does 'moreover' mean?"

"It's a word people like Turner use. I have no idea."

Oswald discarded the Swisher Sweet box, took a bite from the corner of the hologram orders, made to chew it, made a face, spit the paper out, wrapped the remaining cigars in the orders, returned them to his shirt pocket, and then had the idea that he and Bundy should take the equipment just over the hill to the Jacksonville Memorial Gardens and aim it at bereaved men coming out of the viewing parlor until one of them reacted right. In silhouette against the dusking sky, they went over the horizon yanking at each other with the umbilical and cursing and stumbling. Sounds that suggested a fight drifted from their progress.

"And what the hell is contractor's bottom?" one of them said, from the dark.

SKELETON

Mrs. HOLLINGSWORTH HAD MORE doubts about her list, and she was getting tired of them. As 'twere a profanation, she said to herself, recalling the little Donne she knew and liked, of Forrest and the bones of boys—and what about, in sketching these two fond lunatic fools, profaning the memory of the victims of Ted Bundy and indeed—look both ways!—the memory of John Kennedy. What about this?

She put an egg on to think and put eggs on the real list.

It came down to this: how do you profanate the already profane? As much as she detested the craven driving around in their Volvos with their children in crash helmets, there was a reason they were driving around out there like that. Bundy and Oswald were out there littering Wal-Mart parking lots with used Pampers and otherwise trying the burglar bars on their homes. The prisons were full of bad dudes, which was alleged an expression of racism and classism, but it seemed to her, and to the people in the Volvos, that it was an expression of bad dudes knocking people in the head. It was a wreck out there. Forrest had not hidden, and she was hiding, so there be it.

Silly or not, the little love and hope in her golden room over the café were greater than those that operated outside that room in the world outside, or inside, her kitchen. Turner's contractor's bottom was handsomer than the plumber's ass likely to come into her own kitchen if she made a real phone call. She could do nothing about the casualties of war, past or present, and nothing about the souls of the victims of murder, except to entertain herself as best she could while she herself became a spindly skeleton preparing to get into her own uneven grave.

Her Bundy and her Oswald were proving noble in the vigor of their lunatic stupidities. Like any party crashers, they stood a chance of livening things up, if they did not turn out to be utter boors. She was starting to like them, uninvited or not. Where had she got the notion that she could invite, or not, to this party? If to list was to listen, and you listened, you did not speak, you *heard.*

BREAST?

———◦———

ONE MORNING AN EARLY PART of the list caught Mrs. Hollingsworth's eye. She had entered an item called First Breast Not of One's Mother. Why had she not entered an item called, say, First Member Not of the Father? Why would a woman enter a Breast and not a Member? She had written of the man's desire for the woman, and not of the woman's for the man. She could not entertain a section called Member. What Sally thought of Lonnie's tallywhacker, a word it occurred to her Sally might have used back then, for reasons she could not fathom, she had no idea. Had Sally been in love *that way* with Lonnie? She thought so. So why all breast, no glans?

It was as good a thing in the erotic landscape as a tit, certainly, but she did not want to dwell on it. Why would not a fully modern woman want to ponder a penis if she was prepared to dwell on a breast, and in particular on a man's fond apprehension of a breast? Was she a fully modern woman? She hoped not, but this did not convey to her what she was, or what she preferred to be instead. Women had been martyrs, angels, seed vessels, plowhorses, helpmeets, home economists, hearth sweepers, sucklers, stand-by-their-mans, and now were soldiers except for combat and had cell phones in their pants pockets talking worse realtor/CEO goop than their male peers. What was she?

What did it, life, amount to? If you *actualized* yourself, became as talented as you could at what you could, bettered yourself in every way indicated desirable by the arbiters of culture in your surround, well then were you not but a fattened bee among the not so fattened bees all around you, all of you going to buzz along chewing something up and spitting something out until you buzzed no more? *Now this here was a better bee than that one there. See? It's got more a them little hairs on it, like.* Was it going to be better if you had hummed to Mozart?

A breast was a sexier thing than a schlong, is what it amounted to. She kept her list as it was.

TARGET

---◄○►---

—THAT A "BEREAVED" RIGHT THERE, I'd say, Hod. He talkin bout beatin somebody up back inside the funeral home.

—What, that thing hears what they say too?

—I guess. How the hell you gone know they saw Forrest?

—By when they run into the next county if it's anything like what Turner showed us. Hodhawmighty, that *fire* thing was something—

—Yeah, but how you gone know what they thinking? *Why* they runnin, Hod? "Critical part," I recall Mr. Turner saying, and you noddin like a schoolgirl, like you in love with his ass, and now you don't seem to remember what you noddin at.

—I am in love with a man what give me the kind of money we getting for aiming this . . . whatever the fuck it is at people, I confess.

—Say he should beat up a dork in there.

—Who?

—Damned target there, Hod. Hello? You spose dork-beatin-up is a positive character trait for the New Southerner?

—I would think that a outright indispensable trait, Rape. Track on him. I got to pee.

CERTAINTY

—THIS WAS A NICE ROOM.

—Yes. Was?

—I think we should go.

—Why?

—A, because you busted up the floor digging your way in. B, fish can flood into the room, according to you. C, Bundy and Oswald are stalking us, according to you. D, it's about time I consulted the sages on the sward, who will tell us where to go, what to do, in Life, they being Masters.

—E, you're too tired to get up and do anything about Bundy and Oswald; F, how about I was the waitress in that café down there who had precious little else to do but try out a free man upstairs, and did not eat through the floor. That, my friend, is a dumbwaiter patch from yesteryear. My name *is* Sally, but it *wasn't* Sally, if that makes any sense to you.

—That doesn't make any sense to me, Sally not Sally. Don't say those things. They are vicious and cold and true. You clawed through that floor, now miraculously repaired and our best asset, like a nutria after a honeybun, and you were, in some surreal fog that inhabits the better part of my real brain, a girl named Sally with whom I was so purely and gonely in love for a second five hundred years ago that I cannot now afford to remember the moment and hardly the fact but in discrete snatches or curly wisps if you will of that fog, and then a pitchfork tine in my heart, somehow. And then I saw you at my father's funeral and you were new to me but I could not love anymore and so stood dully before you. Isn't this the way it really was—is? Won't you sit on that black-lacquered chair in that orange light and let me behold your *ligne pure?* And can you deny Forrest?

—I never heard it called *that* before. No, I cannot deny Forrest.

—You cannot deny a man you have seen melt into the ground. There are positions and counterpositions in this logical postlogical plausible-deniability world of ours, where the cell phone and blather and the brain tumor rule, but you do not deny that a man has melted into the ground.

—If I sit on the chair, we do not leave the room?

—We do not. The chair, the window, the room, are all we need. And that radiator over there.

FIRST RUN

—WHAT ABOUT THEM OTHER boys there, acryin?

—No no, we want thatn what talkin about beatin up some-body inside a funeral home. That the one, Rape. Something about that *perfect.*

—Ready aim fire gridley, then. Here we go. Forrest, Ride, Rear, Saber, Silent ought to do it. Hodhawmighty, Hod, lookit this.

—Ats bettern the durn demo. *Look* at that sombitch. Sword look like a razor blade. I want me one a them coats he got.

—And look at our boy, Hod. And you right, them others cant even see it.

—He look like he peein his pants.

—And he is stopped talkin bout beatin up people in funeral homes.

—What he sayin?

—He sayin he went one year to Nathan Bedford Forrest High School, which it is very near to here.

—Naw. Is it?

—How the hell *I* know, Hod? All I *do* know is they a man whose somebody done died back in there where he wont to beat somebody up about it, and now he talkin about goin to Forrest High School and peein in his pants.

—Close enough for me. What Turner say we spose to do now we found him?

—*I* dont know, Hod. Why do you keep asking me all these questions? I have run this machine and found our man first one I aimed it at, and you want me to do everthang.

—Read the orders.

—Shit.

—What?

—Where them cigars, Hod?

DEBATE

—◄○►—

THERE WAS SOME DEBATE between Hod Bundy and Rape Oswald as to what to do in terms of bringing their man in now that they had located him. They watched him walk from the funeral parlor to the gravesite, stoop and pick up the Swisher Sweet cigars wrapped in the orders, regard them closely, absently pocket the orders, and momentarily, in a bizarre scene that it seemed only they noticed, they watched the man have the casket opened in the blistering air under the striped awning, talk to the deceased (he said, "Hey, bud," which they knew because Rape Oswald was tracking his every move with the machine), lean into the ornate blue metal-flake box and appear to kiss the deceased, and then slip the cigars into the box with the deceased before signaling for the coffin to be resealed. He stepped back and looked around.

—He lookin to see did anybody see him kiss the corpse, Rape.

—He lookin to see, Hod, where Forrest is.

Then they saw Sally Palmer among the mourners. They said "Hodhawmighty damn" in perfect unison, so that it sounded a little bit like a small choir singing a brief tune.

—*Son!*

—Put that gun on her, Rape. See what *she* knows.

Rape Oswald was so thrown by the beauty of the woman that he could not operate the machine, and they did not determine whether she too could see Forrest. They were both in fact so dazed by her that they had difficulty even following their man from the funeral.

The man led them on an improbable three-state careering into a rented room in Holly Springs Mississippi. There, because they had lost the orders, which had been conceptually as opposed to technically procedural, and because the machine had possibly been damaged by beer in the course of their hauling it three states, they resumed operating the machine with some technical difficulties that had not presented themselves in the successful first run in Jacksonville.

They thought at times that the impossibly beautiful woman they now saw in the window of the rented room was the same one they had seen at the funeral; at other times they were convinced it was a second impossibly beautiful woman.

The competing theories in this domain fought in the minds of Rape Oswald and Hod Bundy like two good dogs. If that sumbitch could find *one* a them purty as at, Rape contended, he could find *two*. It was so impossible that even one woman so beautiful existed that the existence of two women so beautiful did not further strain credulity. The opposing theory was that she had been a waitress in the café below the room. If that the case, Hod Bundy wanted to know, how come she aint still the waitress? She quit, Oswald told him.

She quit, Bundy repeated.

—Ats right.

—She dint quit, because she warnt there in the first place.

—I *saw* him atalkin to this girl in there.

—Well, was she a girl what suck the breath out your yinyang she so purty?

—No. Not as I recall.

—And if it was a girl that good-looking, she would not be here in a café. Hollywood would of come and got her.

—Well, if it's the same girl, how'd she get here? How'd he get her here? He dint even *know* her like, at the funeral.

—That was maybe his strength. That what got her interested in him. It always pays to forget em. Run that thang one more time, Rape. I am heavy bored.

But Rape Oswald could not operate the machine as he looked at the woman, again in the window. Instead he began speaking, in an oddly high voice: Were they a God, Hod, he would not allow the Tyranny of Pussy. He would not, not in no benevolent universe, give boys a dick so hard they make fools of theirself all their life for that right there.

—Give me the goddamn machine, Rape.

—You don't know how to run it.

—You said yourownself they aint no operator's manual.

QUEER FRIENDLYS

———◁◦▷———

—IMONE HAVE TO LOOK at that woman a *long* time, Hod.

—You already looked at her so hard she seen us. Why you wont to keep on?

—I got to see something wrong with her, get some relief. I could get aholt of her, it'd be like when they put Floyd dogs with Maurice bitches. Set a new *pace* in dogs they done that.

—Oswald, you *is* a dog. Take it or leave it, myself.

—What you got against dogs? Dogs is *good*. You worry me, Hod. First the queer friendlys, and now you don't even want *that*—

—The queer friendlys, as you put it, is just reason. It stands to reason some boys might see pussy aint all it's cracked up to be. You said that yourself.

—No, Hod. I said God whupped us with the Tyranny of Pussy, ats—

—Okay, Mr. Buckley. Some boys just said no, like Nancy Reagan said they was suppose to, except they said no to pussy. I don't see why a man need to herniate hisself over that.

—Maybe acause they said yes to dick? Could that be it, Hod? The, like, *Bible* and all?

—Swaggert under his glass table, you mean, telling us what's wrong with queers, paying a girl sit naked on a glass coffee table? You lost your goddamn mind, Oswald. And stop playin with yourself. Whole damn world see you got a rod on.

—I need her.

—Give me the machine.

—You *don't* know how to run it.

—You jack off, I'll take the General out for a walk, see if that girlfriend of yours wants *him* or not.

—I got to look at her a *long* time, Hod. Got to be something wrong somewhere. That the only way you can survive them not wanting you, find the flaw.

—What is Skate?

—Aint no Skate.

—Yeah there is. Saber, Scream, Scour, Skate. I want to see the General can skate.

—Give me that thing.

—No. Set there and play pocket pool and don't mess with me.

—You messing with my hard, Hod.

—Boy, you all *right?*

TONGUE

———◀◉▶———

THE MAN, TIRED ON the bed, recalls the blackened knife his grandmother slapped his father with famously. He did not ever witness that, of course. He witnessed her carving pickled tongue with it, though. She kept entire beef tongues on plates and sliced the tongue meat off and made you a sandwich of it with soft bread and bright, tart, yellow mustard. They were extraordinarily good sandwiches until one day he saw the tongue itself, thick and furry on the plate, and cold, massive. Until that moment he had thought they were eating some kind of composite lunch meat, like Spam, spelled *Tung*. There was in fact a local product called tung oil from a tree called a tung tree, and there was a semipro baseball team called the Tung Nuts that his father had played on, but of this the man as a boy was innocent when he balked at tongue upon his discovery it was not tung.

Bundy has wrenched the ray gun from Oswald, love, the woman said. I believe Oswald is exposing himself to me. It's picking up out here on the square. The nightlife is setting in.

The warm golden light of the room, which was even warmer and more golden as the sun set in the west and shone in the window at this time of day, suddenly flared into something else. It was an electric-feeling light, like that before a tornado, with an odd pastel lilt to its edges, or where it illuminated the edges of things. The black-lacquered chair on which the woman sat looked as if it had been wet with gasoline. A caustic-looking rainbow of color shone from it.

A turbulent tan-colored air pressed up against the window, forcing the woman back from the chair. She had somehow felt a roughness from this air, as if it were strong wind, but it did not appear to be moving, or blowing, much. Nor was it like smoke, though there was a quality of semi-opacity about it. She could still see Bundy and Oswald on the square, though not clearly. Bundy had dropped the ray gun and stood aghast. Oswald was on the ground, masturbating, unless she had altogether lost her senses. She had never seen a man do that on the ground in public. The light made you unsure of things, as if you had taken drugs and now could not be sure whether things were suddenly strange in themselves—this happens, after all—or strange merely in your altered perception of them.

There was a noise almost surflike at the window, loud and abradant. A huge voice sounded outside. It had the impact of bombs, the woman thought. Or perhaps bombs would be sharper, but not as loud, she thought. The voice said, "I'd not have *picked* you wiggers, but you is volunteered, and you, I see, like to ride. Let's us see how well wiggers ride. Mount your boards, boys!" And the roughened air got rougher, and the bombing noises more bombing, and the town dissolved in the brown, tortured, tearing air.

DRIVE-IN

———◁◦▷———

—WHAT THE HELL YOU *DOIN*, Oswald?

—Whippin puddin, what it look like. Better pay attention to your boy Forrest there. Sumbitch biggern a drive-in pitcher show. Looks like the goddamn Wizard of Oz.

—You look like a kid down there. I don't believe you layin there on a sidewalk wanking.

—The mood struck. What, you only do it *in bed?* You romantic?

—I don't do it period.

—Oh. John Effing Kennedy. You are *entirely* fucking with my hard.

Forrest is five stories tall and on a skateboard. His dirty duster is backed up against the window, strafing it when he gestures to the crowd of hundreds of boys in great blooming pedal pushers in the town square. Each holds a skateboard at parade rest. Girls come from the edges of the square and give, each girl to each boy, a silver thimble. "These is non-issue helmets, boys," Forrest says, "like my spurs. They will protect the pinky bone, but only the pinky bone. Your other bones you are to protect yourself at all times. I do not trade in the bones of boys, but some what I know do. So watch yourself. Now mount up. Ride, fist, skull, stomp, gouge, slay, skate!"

The giant leader wheels out first before the improbable parade of gangly and game boys buzzing after him like bees.

SURREAL FOG

‹o›

THE LAST ITEM ON HER LIST sat Mrs. Hollingsworth down for a good hard look at what she was doing. It occurred to her that a woman who entertained herself with a fifty-foot hologram of Nathan Bedford Forrest and a man named Rape abusing himself on a sidewalk was demented. It had come to a point beyond her contemplating setting a plumber on fire, which if she recalled correctly had been the initial engine for all of this. That looked comparatively sane now. What was dementia, she wondered, really? She had always regarded it as a bourgeois slur, a handy putdown of one's mental inferiors that allowed one momentarily to pretend to comprehend mental diseases while doing the put-down. Now, looking at her list, realizing that this is what she had been about, for days now, or weeks, it was tenable that something real was meant by the term—which was Greek, she assumed, after all, so it had to have some root in reality, somewhere, sometime—*dementia.* The Greeks had been solid thinkers, hadn't they? People were or had been demented, and maybe she was one of them. She was now fully *fond* of Oswald and company, Forrest five stories tall, sweeping the land with his boys.

One of her daughters was home, precisely why she could not recall. It was not irregular. One or the other came for a bit and spent most of her time on the phone to the other reporting the deterioration of the home scene. This one, this time, already had phoned the other and said, within impudent earshot, as if she were convinced her mother was deaf or altogether unaware of her surroundings, "She's in some kind of surreal fog." And then, "No, not Lawnboy, she just sits there, *writing.*" "Lawnboy" was a code reference to a scandal involving Mrs. Hollingsworth and the boy who cut the lawn.

This condemnation had nothing to do, Mrs. Hollingsworth knew, with what was actually on this list. That whatever she was doing was *not* a real list—which was clear to anyone who looked at it from across the room, and given the time she spent on it— was sufficient grounds for the surreal-fog charge. She was not making a grocery list, she was not putting on her red ERA coat and selling a house, she was not watching soap operas (real fog? real not-fog? surreal clarity?), she was not housecleaning, she was not dolling up for Dad (whom the daughters despised but felt nonetheless she should seek to please), so she was, ergo, in a surreal fog.

She wondered how these things, her children, had come out of her. How had she borne into the world the Tupperware sisters? And square canisters at that. Her daughters were with the world, with the program. They had gotten aboard the wagon with the rest of the NPR Rockettes. There was a great crowd of folk out there who had assigned themselves the task of watching out for the surreal fog. These were the same folk who thought you were a better person if you could hum along to Mozart. Who elected themselves to all the proprietary boards, local, state, national, and now global, that they could. They were an army of pre-sumers who presumed to legislate what everyone did, thought, felt, should do, should think, should feel. They were the three-headed dog guarding the boat of the sane. They called it, more-over, *being human.* She could see that this was what Forrest was riding against with his boys, who, unable to articulate the evil, could nonetheless dress up against it and slouch against it and ride their insolent sleighs in their insolent pants, showing their asses, over the hills and through the woods to grandmother's house we go. Her daughters looked like the Doublemint twins in this cartoon. They had on matching lime-green sunsuits and cat's-eye glasses and chewed confidently.

Mrs. Hollingsworth was ready to go on a date with Rape Oswald if he came through the door. The Oswald she had left on a sidewalk in Holly Springs Mississippi furiously pulling surreal fog out of himself. She liked his pluck and his mettle. Maybe he was the man for her. To the fog: *en avant!*

And was she demented if she wanted surreal-fog Rape Oswald more than her real-fog husband? There was nothing wrong with her husband, except two things. He was a human being, and after twenty-five years he resided indeed in a fog of familiarity next to her, as she presumed she resided in one next to him. When she had still had friends, she told one of them once, trying to put her finger on just what was wrong between them, "I don't know—he's just so . . . *aloof.*" She had felt ridiculous telling the woman this, watching her tsk her head in an expression of pity suggesting that she did not suffer the same aloofness at her familiar house. It got to where Mrs. Hollingsworth felt self-conscious telling anyone anything, actually, especially these Volvo tsk-tskers, all she or any of them had for friends, and she had gradually obtained an agreeable predicament wherein she did *not* say ridiculous self-conscious things to these women, because she stopped talking to them altogether. Was it demented to have no one to talk to? Or, more precisely, not to want to talk to anyone? She hardly thought so. Was it demented to want an imaginary man? Was that not the condition of all women, starting at about age thirteen? Did they not really keep on doing it all their lives? As did not men keep seeking imaginary women? What was so demented in wanting Rape Oswald if you looked at it this way? He beat hell out of the guy too tired to get off the cot for thinking he had somehow failed his father and because he was no longer in a transport of love, and he *had* the quintessential (imaginary) woman. Or *was* she imaginary? Let us posit she is real, by reason that she is quintessentially imaginary. She is so surreal that she enters a new dimension, of the real. And this woman is then, really, Mrs. Hollingsworth, who is getting tired of Lonnie Schmonnie on the cot and has been making eye contact with the man down on the square who wants her so bad he has swooned to the concrete and risked arrest in the most direct, most natural, least calculated expression of his desire for her that occurs to him. Let us say he is not a human being, even. The NPR Rockettes will not quarrel with that. The Tupperware ladies will admit, "Perhaps he wasn't, um, fully *human.*" Everyone will be very satisfied with that generous consideration of Rape Oswald, on the ground with his need. Cerberus guarding the boat of the sane will bark approval, looking like the RCA dog.

She had worked herself up into a state. She found her daughter, off the phone, and said to her, "Lawnboy and I never slept with each other, love, because he could not contain himself when I kissed him—a young thing who could not leave his mother." Then she went back in the kitchen and removed the phone from the hook so that the girl would have to contain this thickening of the surreal fog by herself for a while. She looked at her prodigious list, her meal for the hungriest largest fool alive. She was in love with the fool who would eat this meal, and digest it, and profit from it, and know what it was.

Forrest was the purest of foolish heroes, riding hard. He was canvas and light, leather and speed, and he did not abide instruction, moral or immoral.

Oswald was the boy. Oswald was the boy listening only to himself, and to her. Oswald was hungry, and a fool, and hers.

SEA CHANGE

———◄○►———

WHEN OSWALD ENTERED THE ROOM, Mrs. Hollingsworth said, "Hi, Ray." He looked at her with a tilt to his head, and then straightened it, as if he had taken her meaning. He had: Rape was a nickname that had done him no good. It had come from a blending of Ray Payne, his first and middle names. A girl in high school had thought his name was Rape Hayne Oswald, and the business had stuck. How the woman handing him the drink she was handing him, in the house in which she was handing it to him, knew his real name, if she did, was beyond him. He was in one of those zones where what you knew, and even what you thought you knew, was far exceeded by what you could not possibly know. He sensed this. It happened more and more to him, rather than less and less, as he perceived was the normal expectation in human life. His had not been the normal life. This losing it agreed with him. There was no profit in saying to someone who somehow knew your real name, "How do you know my real name?" There was so much work involved in determining how she did, if she did—it was possible she *mistakenly* thought this his name, as had the girl in high school thought it else, for example—that he had learned over time not to try. This kind of indeterminacy had been hard for him to accept at first. He had fought it. The fight had given him hemorrhoids, literal and figurative.

So he had a drink in his hand before a nice-looking woman, a scene that was surrounded by no meaningful frame—who she was, why he was here—and he was going with it. She was not the beauty he had recently watched for hire, but no one but that woman was, and his affair with her, conducted alone and on a sidewalk, was over. He pronounced, in fact, just that when he got up off the ground: "Baby, it's been fun, but it's over." And now he was here. He thought he could advise presidents in the matter of conducting their illicit affairs, this recent one of his having been such a model of economy and uncomplication.

A younger woman was emerging from deeper in the house. Showing her the door, the woman who had greeted him said to her, "The immediate forecast is for a deepening of the surreal fog. No need to let the door hit you in the ass." Ray Payne had never heard a woman tell anyone not to let the door hit her in the ass. He liked her—the one speaking. The one leaving was acting somewhat trembly for him.

Seating them in the kitchen, the woman said, "Turner's coming over to dinner. Bring this thing to a head."

"Turner's coming?"

"Yes."

"Bringing Jane?"

"You like Jane?"

"She aint a tire patch on my last girlfriend," he said, "but I will admit her eyes are distracting to a man under the tyranny of . . ."

"Ray, you can speak your mind with me. Under the tyranny of pussy. It's a fair phrase."

This was *precisely* the kind of thing you could not inquire into and still lead a hemorrhoid-free life—how she knew he was going to say that. "I have some questions for Mr. Turner," he said.

"I do too," the woman said. "Like what's to become of Forrest, and what the plan is for the New Southerner."

Ray looked at her hard, started to question, and gave up. Resisting the urge to ask left him in a happy prospect. He recalled a thing a child had told him once: "At the fish market with Mommy I see big flat fish with pimples on them. They are huge and fat and I wish I had never seen them."

He told the woman: "Running the machine was hard. I pressed Thimble and then Melt, without pressing both at once and Control, which I now think was necessary to show the ladies melting the thimbles. It made Forrest talk about thimbles and melt into the ground. My bud Hod thew Forrest fifty foot high and on a skateboard. They is no telling what will become of him. He is indestructible, though. I know that. No matter *what* you push, you get something."

The woman did not bat an eye. She was in the zone too, apparently. "I know all that. But what about the new boy who would save the South?"

117

"Dweeb with the girl?'

"Yes. Man on the bed."

"He a pistol ball."

"You liked that woman, didn't you?"

"You know, my bud Hod took exception to a man pleasuring hisself over her, and he all the time saying these Queer okay, I'm okay things. He got something against kids, *dogs* . . . I don't know about him."

"You don't need him."

"I *know* I don't need him."

"Ray, do you have a headache?"

"Headache?"

"John F. Kennedy told Harold Wilson that he, John F. Kennedy, got a headache if he didn't have a woman every three days."

"Oh, *that* kind of headache. John *Effing* Kennedy."

"Let me get a smell of you, Ray, see about fixing that headache of yours."

"Smell me? You want to smell me?"

"Ray, at this point in life, everyone can more or less run his equipment. It's what a man *smells* like, not what he *does*. I about know what you are going to *do*."

In the action that followed in the bedroom, Ray had occasion to think of the rest of what the child had told him about the fish: "They are ugly and very weird. I do not like them." There was an element of that in sex, Ray thought. Part of it was ugly and weird and not likable, but the firestorm of hormones kept you liking it. He and the woman wrestled well together, it seemed, for a first time. She seemed very comfortable with him. He entered a fog of

118

flesh and got lost in her for a while. When he emerged, looking for air, he found her gasping too, saying, "Hodhawmighty damn. *Son!*" This was somewhat like hearing her tell the other woman not to let the door hit her in the ass—he had only ever heard a man say "hodhawmighty" and "son" that way. Yet it struck him as perfectly correct and fitting. He felt he had known this woman all his life.

When Turner and Jane got there, they sat down to dinner, and the woman who was familiar to him now in two ways got right to it. She said to Turner: "The man too tired to get up from the bed for fantodding all the live-long day about failing his father, even though Helen of Troy is in the room with him, has now decided that his problems with his father stem from not going out for the track team in the tenth grade when a coach at Nathan Bedford Forrest High School invited him to. That was the invisible point of failure, he now thinks. He can't understand why he did not go out, other than that he did not like to run for its own sake, and his conviction that the coach was a sadist or pederast of some sort, which does not seem to him now sufficient grounds for disregarding the coach. Is this man, immobile on a bed in a rented room in Holly Springs Mississippi, truly the New Southerner?"

Turner looked at the woman and at Ray. "Oswald indicates he is the only man they found who was properly undone by the visions of Forrest."

"He the only one we showed him to," Ray said.

"Helen of Troy?" Jane said. "She isn't a patch on me." At this

Ray snorted. She turned to him. "What? You don't think my eyes are special? Have you seen the post-partum workout video?"

The woman cut in: "Your eyes are special, but you are not Helen of Troy. No one is. That is what 'Helen of Troy' means. Now excuse us. We are about something important here. Your husband here is engaged in a large project doomed to failure, and I want to wrap this up by making sure he knows that."

Ray was delighted with all of this. His imprudent confession that they had only one candidate for Turner's New Southerner was apparently to go unpunished, unnoticed even. He was free to fiddle about the table, stealing little looks at Jane, whose eyes indeed suggested fried blue marbles but who did not, all in all, incline him to the ground with the hurt of need. The woman his hostess seemed to have fixed that somehow anyway. For this he was grateful. He had had to throw himself to the ground with the hurt of need nearly all his life, which had once seemed an onerous thing, but which now did not because of the inexplicable sensation he had in the presence of his hostess that he had not been alive all that long—"nearly all his life" seemed somehow a laughably short time. This was a curious sensation to have, sitting there in obvious middle age, wondering if he should have his hair styled as Turner did, or if going to the Barber College and getting these whitewall specials for five dollars from tentative students and looking like he'd been treated for mange with foo-foo water was good enough anymore in the modern world. He had a feeling of being really out of it, there with Turner and Jane and this woman drilling Turner as if she owned him. He wanted suddenly not to be out of it.

"Why does the black man take to the cell phone so hard?" he suddenly asked Turner.

Turner turned to him naturally and began speaking without pause or seeming interruption from whatever he had been saying to the woman. "I'm glad you have asked me that question, Oswald. I can answer it. The black man cannot own the land, we have seen to that. He does not want the water. He once wanted the road, but that really was a wanting of the land. When it was Cadillacs, he managed. Now that it is the BMW, the Black Man's Wish, he can't. He now wants the air. From the beginning he wanted the air. This is why he got loud. This is why he carried the ghetto blaster. He virtually invented the sub-woofer. And now he can take command of satellites with the cell phone. He is equal in this respect to the whitest of white men, the astronaut. Were the market share any larger, a man would be fiduciarily negligent unto himself not to market a gold-colored phone exclusively for the brother."

Ray was impressed at Turner's smooth delivery. He thought it might be good to learn to speak that way himself, and he certainly would have to consider it if he began wearing his hair in a way that made people expect that kind of sound to come out of a man. He thought he might, what the hell, try it right now: "These ideers might appear in congress with my haircut, sir, as far as blow-dry. I have oft pondered, moreso, moreover, why the brother does not have his own entire industries—a national bank, for example. Prioritizing the brother. For all the fay-the-fair made about his soul food, one does too see a dearth of restaurants in the brother's name, and certainly there is no national chain. And you would know best the opportunities in mass communications, which it has already brought us wrassling on TV and colored black-and-white movies. I mean, why should not the brother have not merely his own phone but his own network? His own satellites, even?"

Turner looked at him in astonishment. "We have discussed these things in bunkers," he said. "As part of the planning for the New South. You might be more of the team than I knew. Do you want to be more of the team than I knew?" At this, Turner began weeping. It was a quiet, not very disturbed weeping, which suggested as many positive emotions as negative, Ray thought, rather as women may cry when they are happy fully as often, and often as fully, as when they are sad. Jane seemed also not much bothered by it, and made ready with a napkin as if to hand it to Turner momentarily when he came up for air. Ray fingered the raw spots of his haircut and thought, Really.

He discovered that the hostess had left the room and was now returning with dessert on a tray. It looked very good, especially since he could not recall their having had anything else. It was not that he was particularly hungry, it was merely that this was the first food they had seen, and it looked particularly fetching for that reason alone. He jumped up to help the woman with the tray, saying to her, "Honey child!" This came out of his mouth as oddly as a small toad. The woman took no exception to the toad, in fact winked at him. She glanced at Turner. "We are coming along nicely," she said. Then to him, "You're a good boy."

This compliment went into Ray as true as a pang on the pan of his heart. It had not been said to him in a long, long time. It made him want the woman again, in the bedroom, and soon. "I'm a voodoo chile," he said.

"That you are," the woman said. "Now watch this."

The curtain behind Turner opened. An image began to obtain, not unreminiscent of the way the *Star Trek* boys beamed into place, or the way closed-circuit TV sometimes grainily gathered itself in the early days of closed circuitry. "The artist Degas could talk any woman he wanted into taking her clothes off and bathing in front of him, apparently," Ray said.

The woman said, "Shh."

On the screen Forrest appeared, hair shining, blowing in a wind. Violins blowing a violin wind. Moss blowing in a wind. Sir Walter Scott shook hands with Forrest. A guillotine tumbled by on the wind. "The French were of no help to us," Forrest said. A rich and resonating accentless male voice-over intoned: ". . . and the Ku Klux Klan, under Forrest's orders, having served its purpose, was disbanded in 1872. It wudn' a black thang." This *Frontline* voice saying "wudn' a black thang" made Ray laugh out loud. Then Forrest said, "Its mission, which was not to terrorize the Negro, was fulfilled." Forrest appeared to be distracted. Ray had not seen him so before. He was fidgeting with his person, patting about himself as if checking for personal property in his pockets. The marvelous canvas coat was there, in its perfect disorder: dirty and yet spectral, rucked-up and shot and torn and yet whole and sturdy and rugged as armor. Ray wanted a coat like that.

Some kind of commercial intervened in the filmstrip, or whatever it was. Ray had not heard the term "filmstrip" in a long time.

He had not actually heard it now. It had been heard, he guessed, by his brain. The commercial was for Ronson lighter fluid. Ray had never seen a commercial, or any other kind of advertisement, for Ronson lighter fluid.

"Ronson lighter fluid exists independently of the exigencies of commerce," Ray said aloud, and they all told him by quiet gesture to be quiet. "And those yellow cards with the little red flints," he pressed on, "they don't have to advertise *that*." They shushed him.

Forrest returned, his hair on fire. He was saying something indistinguishable. It sounded like "Someone get the phone," but Ray thought what he was saying was cleverly designed to sound like indistinguishable talk. That is to say, you could decide what he was saying for yourself and be no more inaccurate than your neighbor, because Forrest was not saying anything at all. They had cleverly effected this phenomenon. It *sounded* like talk but wasn't. It was like some poetry.

Ray closed his eyes. He wanted to see Forrest ride. He almost wanted to run the machine that projected him again himself, because Forrest was not doing interesting things here in this professional film or whatever it was. Forrest could ride, fist, skull, stomp, gouge, pistol ball in hip, mercury pouring from his feet where his thimble spurs melted back onto the fingers of the fair ladies who hoped for him

and loved him and loved then, still, too, themselves

and the woman was on him again, the fog of flesh that was her and that was him was on them again, and she was saying "Are you hungry?" and he was saying "Yes, ma'am, I am hungry," and she smiled at him, a sweet smile that took a long time and made him feel like . . . what? . . . as if she were laughing at something, at him, but she was not, and she said "And are you a fool?" and he said "Oh, *yes,* ma'am, I am a fool," and she said "Then you are a hungry fool?" and he said nothing because it was obvious that he was, and the woman smiled again the long smile that made you think she was finding something funny about you but she was not.

REAL FOG

————◀◦▶————

WHEN MRS. HOLLINGSWORTH RETURNED from her dinner with Turner and Jane and Ray and the irrepressible unre-
doubtable Forrest, as fine as an immortal graying hound, she felt
marvelously refreshed and simplified. She felt she had traveled to
a wonderful place, a sentiment that was suspiciously brochure-
sounding but that she had no trouble holding anyway. I went to
a place and I enjoyed it very much, she said to herself. Now that
she was "back"—and she had some reservations about that ter-
minology too, because she sensed you did not come all the way
back and you did not ever really leave, somewhat as with taking
acid—she kept smacking her lips for some of that place again.

Here she was again in what her daughters would call, she
supposed, the real fog—no, they wouldn't, they were not that
bright—and it looked immeasurably worse. The newspaper
contained an item, among all the murders and barricadings and

shooting sprees, about the curvature of the president's member. He had a peyroni that did not, she read, get fully erect. The president of the United States. This was real. Tell her this was not also then a fog, and a worse one than the one she had learned to take lodgment in.

She had got to see a media mogul cry—where else might you see that? And he had wept so ambiguously, so endearingly, so unselfpityingly. She was already ready to go back. A phrase was toying with her head. She had had more of the phrase than she had now, and it had been better, meant more than the fragment of it she now possessed. She had lost part of the phrase in the collision with the real fog. The president's limber peyroni had whapped it out of her head. Everyone could be Coleridge, she supposed. This was why They had taken laudanum away from us, wasn't it? They did not like us all being Coleridge. If she were caught selling laudanum from the back of a Volvo, she would do more time than if she shot someone.

What remained of the toying phrase was only this: "in the ghost of her lies." Something something *in the ghost of her lies.* Maybe *In the ghost of her, lies* something something. No: the original meaning was along the lines of the phantom of her prevarications. The phantom of her prevarications, the ghost of her lies—she was in love with the ghost of her lies, her ghostly lies, and she would return to him, and to them, when she could. There was nothing quite like the clarity of the surreal fog when you came out of the muddy real.

For the rest of her life she would shop, for herself and for whatever hungry fools came by to partake of her improbable food. This resolve filled her with so much cheer that she hatted up and headed out to the real store for some probable food. Waked up, part of her vision intact, the ghost of her lies in her purse, she was not altogether in despond. She Volvoed forth into the real fog.

BLUEBERRIES

———◦———

AT THE GROCERY STORE Mrs. Hollingsworth found herself stopped at a long chest freezer containing packaged vegetables and fruits. The handsome simulations of the vegetables and the fruits on the packages drew the eye agreeably to their gay colors through the calming fog of frozen air hovering over them. She stood there, absently handling this and that. She rarely bought any frozen food of this sort, precisely because the packaging was so nice she felt it had to conceal something fraudulent. She was aware that frozen food had passed out of middle-class favor and was now a food of the lower classes. But there was a brand of bulk vegetables from Georgia of the country-people sort—cut green beans and okra and field peas—sold in two-pound undecorated clear plastic bags that she would buy. These vegetables were good, and they interested her because all it said on the bag, virtually, was "Moultrie, Georgia," as if that would, or should,

131

be enough to sell the food in the bag. And it was. All the other frozen produce, in full-tilt packaging, which she thought of as emanating actually from Hollywood, turned out to be from a subsidiary of a subsidiary of a subsidiary of Coca-Cola or General Motors, in Battle Creek or Stamford or who knew where.

She imagined Forrest riding in here and laying in a plain bag of cut okra for each saddlebag, to pop in his mouth like popcorn all day through a long fight. She actually looked around for him, realizing as she did that she looked exactly like the man on the bed's grandmother, who would slap children's hands to protect her pickled tongue, the time she escaped from her nursing home and petered out in the sunny foyer of an apartment building two blocks away, saying to passing strangers whom she mistook to be her rescuers, "What took you so long?" The old children-knife-slapping poker queen mistook each passerby to be a saber-slapping Forrest. Mrs. Hollingsworth had that same desperate lost hopeful look standing there with a bag of okra in her hand. She put it down. Forrest could do a lot, but rescuing her in here was not one of the things he could do.

She beheld, next to the okra she had put down, a box of blueberries. She knew that the box itself was plain, gray, thin cardboard folded together none too sturdily; what shored the affair up was a perdurable waxed paper well sealed around the box, a light unwettable paper as nice as good wrapping paper, and this delicate slippery material held the coarse, loose box of berries together, a kind of intimacy she found sexy. The wrapper was pure white, and on it was printed a prospect of blueberries that looked like no blueberries on earth, or none that anyone on earth had ever seen, at any rate. They were cold-looking and "garden-moist," the wrapper proclaimed, a remarkable effect given that the blueberries she'd seen had looked like hot purple peppercorns. These Hollywood berries were princely, each with its dainty spiked crown. The photograph did what Van Camp's or General Motors or AT&T or whoever asked of it: made the human being want to eat blue food, an improbable thing in his general habit.

In the portrait of these surreal blueberries, Mrs. Hollingsworth saw the man on the bed get up from it and look around and see that the impossibly beautiful woman was gone. This perception on his part put a waft of momentary desperation through him, followed hard by a waft of determination to endure the loss of the woman. Sexual deprivation quickens the step, Mrs. Hollingsworth thought, seeing the sentiment penciled over the scene as if it were one in a comic strip. It *was* a comic strip, she thought then. She had no trouble with that. She herself was comic.

She saw the man put on a crisp new shirt of a plaid fabric so thin it could be seen through. He dropped the tissue and the straight pins from the shirt packaging onto the hard golden floor of the room. It was the first time anything—even Helen of Troy's clawing through it—had detracted from the stunning perfection of the floor. The momentary carp flowing over it had no more marred it than fish mar water. The pins and the tissue fell to the floor and stayed where they fell, the shiny glints of the pins random and vaguely dangerous, the crumpling of the paper humanly messy. They were harbingers of something, Mrs. Hollingsworth thought. She loved that word. They were harbingers.

The man stepped lively onto the street. He had complemented the hick shirt with a pair of pants too short to conceal his brogans and white socks. He looked a perfect clodhopper. She liked him very much. She had not liked him much lately. Now that he was out of his moony phase he was looking okay. He had determined to get himself a job, any job, that day, right there in Holly Springs Mississippi. That was pluck. He wasn't going to get a job that day, or probably any other day, in Holly Springs Mississippi, where he knew no one, and even he knew it, but that did not stop him or Mrs. Hollingsworth from seeing the possibility of it. What mattered was that he was taking himself in hand—this resolve was fairly pinned on him, like a blue ribbon he'd been conferred at 4-H. He'd won the prize for Taking Himself in Hand.

The impossible job he would not get that he would somehow get would be on the order of the lowest hand at the feedstore. He would carry fifty-pound bags of feed and fertilizer and seed to pickup trucks while his superiors at the store, some of them much younger than himself, handled the transactions at the counter. These would involve a total figure that was rarely particularized, a check that was never questioned, and some talk about cutworms, or bots, rust, whatever the hell the new rot-thing or bug was; the county agent might know, might not, would pretend to until it was too late. Was it true sixteen-gauge shells was going to disappear? No, not that we heard, anyway. What is this shit about not being able to vaccinate your own dog for rabies? I don't know, that's what they say. Well, they ain't worth the powder it'd take to blow them.

The man lately from the bed would grunt all day beneath his

loads in paper and burlap sacks, some of which smelled good enough to eat. A thick-necked, thick-shouldered high school football player, traditional holder of his position at the feedstore, would one day beat him up behind the feedstore. Or, more precisely, two other football players, on behalf of the jobless football player, themselves without feedstore aspirations, would beat him up. Whoever did it, they would not realize that the wild and lucky moves the man came up with in the hopeless defense of himself were inspired by fear. They would see only that he had the balls and the surprising skill to somehow nick them and so would not extinct him altogether but would leave him there and say, "Go on in there and tote your bags, old man," and the man would notice that, wing them or not, he had not disturbed even the Skoal tucked in their lips. No one after this would ever bother the man again.

He crossed the street now in his red-plaid highwater nattiness and approached the council of elders in their herringbone and suspenders. They regarded him without cheer. He said to them, "Wondering where I might find work."

They appeared not to have heard him. Finally one of them— the man could not tell which one—said, "Woik. *Heah?*"

"Yes."

The elders looked off with far and indifferent gazes, each in a different direction away from the man, as if they expected something more interesting to appear over the horizon.

Mrs. Hollingsworth put the blueberries back down into the surreal fog of the freezer and left the store without buying the blueberries or the okra or anything at all. It was acceptable, leaving the grocery store empty-handed, the odd time.

HOME

———◁◦▷———

WHEN SHE GOT HOME purchaseless from the store, nosing the Volvo through some boys on her street whom she had difficulty regarding as the backbone of Forrest's final command, particularly given the horrendous postures of the boys, Mrs. Hollingsworth retook her kitchen, headquarters for her recent lovely campaign. The house had a thick and palpable quiet to it that was almost frightening; it allowed you to *smell* its emptiness. This stillness and smell of emptiness and quiet ticking space had in fact frightened her before her visit to the wonderful place of the list, before her list-making ride with Forrest. Now there was something thrilling about it, a challenge to defy it.

Something final had occurred as she held the blueberries just above the cool fog of the freezer. "I guess I had a goddamn epiphany," she said to her egg pot, and put an egg on to boil. She understood that she had come to use this little gesture, boiling an egg, as a signal that she could, at will, cook a real meal.

There had been nothing like cooking that other one, though. Ray Oswald had saved her life—she tried that out in her mind, observed the hysterical stripe down it, like the line of white down a skunk, and thought the little skunky idea was fine. She had gone to a marvelous, improbable, at times profane and silly place, and it had been just what she needed. There was not a lot to be said for replacing your uncorrupted dull daily waste of living with a corrupted vital imaginary escape from it, perhaps, but it was a fact that she and others around her were living in stilled and stilted timid toadspawn conformity, afraid of something they could not identify except in particulars—their burglar bars, their life insurance policies, their options-weighing at every moment of their lives. This was a fearful fetid nothingness she could do nothing about. She had at least not escaped into the talk shows, or into part-time commercial self-actualizing (a 6 percent commission on a house made you whole), or into swooning at the disorders of environment management. She thought it funny how the poor environment had been raped just fine until there was a sufficient excess of the people who had effected the raping to produce sufficient numbers of themselves who were sufficiently idle that they might begin to protest the raping of the environment, which was irretrievably lost to the raping by that point. And this would be the great soothing cathedral music, the stopping of the chainsaws amid the patter of acid rain, that all good citizens would listen to for the quarter-century it took them all to wire up into cyberspace and forget about the lost hopeless runover gang-ridden land, reproducing madly still all the while, inside their bunkers listening to NPR. She wondered what Forrest might make of these tree and owl rebels. Forrest was the only man on earth who could ride against the forces of the NPR, stop the music of antidoom, tell them the music wasn't going to cut it, they were doomed before the first idler picked up the first fiddle. Jesus been hard on all you, she could hear him say.

But she knew he wasn't interested in that, because she wasn't interested in that. The root cause of no trees left was no people to say too many people. And that was because, by hysterical reasoning, the Civil War had been lost, the Union perfected, and the perfect Union meant the most populous one you could make. Once the one population got on everyone's nerves, as it had, it was a simple logical matter to assert the good of *other* populations; hence the loud, swiveling, clarion call extolling the endless virtues these days of what had come to be called, in exquisite euphemism, in the speech of the realm, diversity. Forrest had not meant to stop this nonsense, because he had not—no one had—had the sense to see nonsense like it coming, or even to conceive it, way back then when people were still sane, shooting each other over Sir Walter Scott.

She got her egg, cooled it in a stream of tapwater, and sat down to eat it. The man now up off the bed who had lost the most beautiful woman in the world and not got a job carrying grain and seed to be beaten by high school boys and ignored by old men was the man for her, after all. He was wounded, and none too custodial of his wounds, but who was any better? Her head was no clearer than his, his no more fogged than hers. In the surreal fog she could see him ask a plain woman to a real dance in Holly Springs Mississippi and begin again.

She drew a hot bath. She had found this was a tonic thing to do in the middle of the day, especially if you ran the water too hot and allowed yourself plenty of time to waste in it. She traipsed around naked, ostensibly collecting little bath necessities, a little Clinique this in a bottle the color of a stinkbug, the *eau de* that in cut glass, a German boar-bristle brush with a nice waxed wood handle that felt much better to your hand than the bristle did to your skin. She did not need or want these things. She wanted only the good heat and the water and her calmed mind. She got in the bath.

The water was hot enough to make her wonder if she should let it cool—perhaps she was herself a giant human egg set to boil—but stepping out of a tub once in it is a hassle greater than burning yourself, so she slipped on in. The determination was good. She was level with steam coming off the water. It went over the surface of the water like miniature clouds, which is what it was. She moved these small clouds about gently with her hands. The clear, unbroken water under them was perfect and beautiful.

She suddenly wanted a lemon beagle. The prospect of this yellow-and-white dog was vivid—a washed-out-looking gentle thing that hunted rabbits with great passion and even greater skill but meant no harm to rabbits. She was not sure if you called it a lemon beagle or a lemon-and-white. To lie in a scalding tub of water in the middle of the day in a transport of steam and want a dog she had not thought of or seen in maybe thirty years, and have this be the dominant want in her heart at this moment— was she trivial? Was she merely idle?

She entertained this thought: she was losing her way. Was she losing her way? The question presumed she had once not been losing her way. Had she once not been losing her way? She thought it obvious that all people, or virtually all, must for a time be convinced they know their way. It has not yet occurred to them that they do not know their way, to be more precise. Then at some point it does occur to them. They may suddenly, or gradually, feel that they do not know their way, and they may then be able to doubt that they ever actually did know it. Given the condition they suddenly find themselves in, they wonder what species of hoodwink convinced them they ever thought they knew what was going on. They had merely trotted along, confident and doglike, as people do, full of pride and certainty and ambition and their little educations, as people are supposed to. And some of them, like Mrs. Hollingsworth, come to a halt. In a tub, in a store, in a kitchen, in making a list of real things, in making a list of surreal things, in cooking for a sane man or cooking for a fool.

She thought again about the place she'd been. Was there a fool it would nourish, real or not? What if the fool it would nourish was only the cook? The cook who lay under small hot gambols of surreal fog the idle live-long day wanting a bleachy yellow dog? Not wanting even, perhaps, probably, a real dog but just this prospect of a dog? No damned shed hair and Volvoing it to the vet where the labels on a vaccine read like computer applications and cost as much. She just wanted a *dog*.

So maybe she should just *cook*. Cook the fool's meal for herself, the fool cook. Then she saw the man who had left the bed and been left by the woman, who had been beaten by the boys and been left by the boys. He was in his cheap red plaid shirt, sober and alone. Anyone else on earth in that shirt was not sober and was not alone.

He was puzzling in the realm of his father and his father's mother. Mrs. Hollingsworth could not tell what he was after. He did not know himself, perhaps, probably. She was tired of that: "perhaps, probably." She'd make it "perbly."

Perbly he was wondering how his father could be a football hero and go to war and have been slapped with a knife by his mother and still love his mother, when he the son would not even go out for track, yet would run from war, or a street fight for that matter, and did not kiss his own mother beside her very grave. Perbly something like that. He had somehow come to be a bleached-out yellow dog, afraid even of love, if we are to judge from his travail with Sally and Helen of Troy, perbly Sally's later incarnation.

Perbly he was waiting for someone to cook him a fools meal. She was tired of perbly. He *was* waiting for a meal. He was waiting to be transformed into a man. He was waiting for Forrest to ride by and ask him if he wanted to go out for track, so to speak. It had been at Forrest High School, after all, that he first deigned not to participate, fearing a little pain in the legs. The legs had been good enough to attract the coach, whether the coach was a pederast or legitimate. He should have tried the coach, either way. For whatever reason, or complex of reasons, real or surreal, novel or not, that Mrs. Hollingsworth could dream up or not, that were to be found in her brain or in her heart or were not in either place and were possibly in some *real* place, the moment he did not regard the coach as a man is the moment he lost his way. Mrs. Hollingsworth was a woman who had lost her way.

The man was getting his legs back by carrying sacks of grain. When Forrest came by, he would need nourishment to accept whatever role Forrest offered him—stopping in a leather-creaking surge of horse stink and steel, saying, "You aint no relation to Bragg or Floyd, saddle up, you want to fight. Put that hound dog in a saddlebag. We could *use* some rabbit," and gone in a blur of saber and canvas and horse snort and clenching rump.

Mrs. Hollingsworth would cook. She would be the campaign cook. That night Forrest would not remark of the food. He would never talk of food. He would say, "Picked up a boy with a yellow dog today. Dog looked like a ghost of a dog. Boy about the same. Boy looked like a Floyd. Hope to God he aint. Dog look like a damn lemon. Don't nobody tell that Jackson character we got us a lemon dog." There would be a round of chuckling, some polite and some earnest, at this levity.

Mrs. Hollingsworth made some notes in the air over the steamy water:

1. The levity of the doomed has no equal.

2. Only the airspace at Appomattox is original, where it was. The floor is not the floor they trod, the window not the window that admitted the light on the document they signed. The light is not the same, but it is in the same place. The *space only* is truly preserved.

3. All those fraudulent bricks. Only 4 percent of them original, and none of them in the right place.

4. All those fraudulent men. What if they *all* came through the door? Who was she waiting for? If Forrest himself came to dinner, would she not find fault even with him? Would she not say, No, General, you are lying: it *was* a black thing, to the bone. And Forrest would say, Ma'am, you been listening to too much Yankee radio. Man could handle the NVA, but I be God if he can fight the NPR. It's too many of em. Hell, they bout brought down Lincoln hisself, only straight-thinking sober man they had.

And this would be funny, and true, and she would like this Forrest for a moment. But then what? Then did not the old torment begin? And what was the old torment? The old torment was that she was alone now because she had been afraid to be alone when young. And, afraid to be alone young, she had made herself into the contemporary companion to whoever was at hand and handy. She had not made herself into herself. She had made herself into a model companion for other people who themselves were not waiting to become themselves but who were also modeling for companionship. So they had all become model companions.

It went without saying that she had not waited for the person she might have loved, either. So it was not surprising that now, when her station in life suggested she was mature and sane, she was dreaming of wildly improbable men like a schoolgirl. Well beyond a schoolgirl: she was in a scalding tub of water in the throes of bourgeois idleness dreaming up the most ornery sonsofbitches she could. She had lost her mind. It was fortunate that that did not matter. There were certainly so many excess idle minds about that it did not matter if a few, or a lot, strayed. She could fire out of this tub and make chicken cacciatore and Jell-O and plan a dinner party and buy some symphony tickets and sell a house and do Jane's video workout, or not. Not looked right.

OSWALD

———<o>———

My EXISTENCE IS FAIRLY TENUOUS, if you would have no objection to a man called Rape, whose demeanor and rhetoric thence would not allow you to anticipate it, using such a word. My tenuosity (there, that's better, isn't it?) is in fact what allows me to be, well, tenuous even in speech. I am in one sense but a figment, and a figment is nothing if not unstable. I can as easily, at her whim, say, "I only exist, you want to put it that way, by just keepin on keepin on."

I am fortunate she likes me, or liked me. It came to that rather capital evening in which I got to eat with Jane and sleep with the hostess. It was a heady evening. No one could have predicted Turner crying like that. There are two explanations for that, or let us say one explanation in two forms: he was under considerable pressure, and everybody has their limit.

She was hot, I can say that. She got what she wanted out

of me, and done quit me. That is not a behavioral pattern in women with which I am unfamiliar with it. They regular animals it comes to getting what they want. They have learned to weep and coo to mask it. We buy it. Or let me elevate that: enthralled within the tyranny of desire, we pay all our cash and then apply for credit. We see no practical end to what we will pay. The pedestal philosophy was a shrewd business intended to get the lioness off the ground. Give us some time to lick ourself in between rounds, in other words, moreso, so to speak, per se—I can be as ridiculous as you please. She preferred me that way, and I cannot maintain I mind it altogether. The labor of being colorful does not exceed that of being sane.

But I would have you note that she prefers the other old boy to me, a matter on which even she is clear. This should surprise no one. To my publicly masturbating, a scene she lifts from one in her own life that she witnessed at a mental health hospital, over the unattainable and ineffably beautiful woman she tyrannized me with—I the only man articulate enough to come up with "tyranny of pussy," therefore the one to pay—she prefers and allows numbnut's *having* the woman, first, and then his lying there in a contemplative fugue so long he loses her. He loses her because he shows evidence that he is not fully under the tyranny of desire. He gets away, as it were. So it is he who must be pursued. I am thrown a cursory sexual favor, fed, given a bad haircut, and dismissed. There is nothing end a shaky relationship like a bad haircut in my experience, in other words.

But cot boy, he gets off with a bad shirt. He limps on. She don't know exactly where he's at. He don't either—to be precise, she would have you *believe* he doesn't know what he is about. I have other information on this, which I will not share. Suffice it to say, before I leave here—which I am doing it as quick as I can (because after you have seen me sleep with the master you are not going to see me masturbate on a sidewalk again, which was not as fun as it looked)—that cot boy finds the labor required to be in a father dither and mother muddle and life limbo to not exceed that of being undithered, unmuddled, and walking tall.

I believe it a tenable proposition that people in books or life do not do more work than is required of them.

DATE

———◆———

GIVE ME SOME OF YOUR foo-foo water, lieutenant. I have a date. Should I go acourtin when Grant is out there at large? No, I should not. If that sumbitch is drunk, hope to God he don't sober up. They'd a had his butt in charge sooner we'd be resting now. Wrong people fought this thing, lieutenant. Saved ourself some boys, we could have been bettern what we were. Got to go to this address here in Holly Springs. I'll ride over alone. It's a note on this purple paper, parfumy.

Find out what that new boy's name is. Worries me. Still think he might be a Floyd, even a Buckner. Come up to me today with that lemon dog and a brace of rabbit he'd got, and I congratulated him, you know, and suddenly the fool is saying, "General, my daddy didn't even teach me how to play *cards.*" All I could do not to laugh.

Lieutenant, I confess the boy had me stumped there. I had

to resort to the Leader Act. I leaned down to him and looked at him with the electric fightin eye and said, deep-like, "Boy, I'mone teach you how to play cards and *raise God.*" Boy fell back teary and grateful from the horse like I'd done christened him. Made me blush. This Leader thang get on your nerves. I sprung off before it got any worser Make sure he aint a Floyd—or related to *anyone* in command.

How you tie these things? Women. I wouldn't even go if people wouldn't say maybe I'm gettin like Davis and Bragg. Don't wait up. You in charge. Anything happens, fight. That don't work, run.

FRUGGING WITH FORREST

————◦————

WHEN FORREST COMES IN THE DOOR, Mrs. Hollingsworth is wearing the same cologne he got from his lieutenant. She and Forrest smell so much alike they are put at ease and think themselves more familiar with each other than they are. Mrs. Hollingsworth has Jimi Hendrix playing, loud. Mrs. Hollingsworth is moving about in a strange, contortional way. "Do you frug, general?"

"What *is* that shit?" Forrest says, holding his ears.

Mrs. Hollingsworth begins laughing hysterically at this. Forrest himself begins to laugh. He has a slightly impish look unlike any Mrs. Hollingsworth has heretofore conceived. She has only seen the grim look and the electric look. He is putting her on!

He has picked up the Hendrix album cover. "I be damn."

Mrs. Hollingsworth decides this business will be funny but predictable, and cuts it off.

"Have a seat, general."

Forrest takes an order as well as he gives one. He notices the fabric of the sofa. It is a nubbly nylon that is utterly alien to his hand. He passes his hands absently over it for some time. Mrs. Hollingsworth has time to regard him: a man who will have fought so hard that he will wither away once this conflict is over and die, of nothing more certain than atrophy, at age fifty-six. A man this strong who can collapse.

"General, have you found the woman you love?'

"That has never occurred to me."

"Does it interest you?"

"No, it does not. Not the way you put it."

"Why not?"

"I don't know."

"That's not a bad answer."

"That's a relief."

"General, you mock me."

"Ma'am, why not?"

"That's not bad either."

"Well, we all do-si-do then."

While it was true that she could do with Forrest what she wanted, it was also not true. He was difficult. But this too, his difficulty, she had given him, she thought. She wasn't sure. The uncertainty was thrilling. He did not need a nurse—a peculiar man, in this respect. She had not known a man who did not need a nurse. The only man she could have imagined before this who did not need a nurse was a dead man. And the dead man would have needed a nurse, desperately, right up until he died.

The proposition of having a man who did not need you was a bit frightening. It should not be, but it was. The thing she thought she had failed at was precisely this: waiting for the man who did not need her but wanted her. She had been afraid to wait for that, then, and when she saw it before her, now, the thing itself, it too scared her. Perhaps she was merely afraid of everything. Most people, she thought, were, and she was perhaps finally not any better. It had been pretty to think so, she thought. A woman was not to be faulted for her pretty thoughts.

"Is a woman to be faulted for her pretty thoughts, general?"

"That has not occurred to me either," Forrest said.

Mrs. Hollingsworth realized why she had summoned the general. "General, could you send that boy with the lemon dog over tomorrow, if you are not fighting?"

Forrest looked at her directly. He understood and accepted her rejection. His hand continued to move sensually on the sofa, feeling the fabric. "Sho I can do that, ma'am—that is what general means. What kind of hide is this?"

"Hide?" She then understood him to mean the fabric on the sofa.

"I don't want to see whatever you skunt this off of," Forrest said. "Or hunt it."

"General, are you tired?"

"I'm tireder than a dog lying underneath another dog."

NOR NURSE NOR NEED

———◄○►———

THE MAN IN THE PLAID SHIRT came into the house like something hunted and hunting. He was nervous and deliberate. Mrs.
Hollingsworth could see that she had complicated him to a point
that was not easy for him. He was hurt in some way that he did
not wish to acknowledge; he felt that if he did, it would confirm
and solidify and even deepen the hurt. There was an aura about
him that, like Forrest's hologram, showed a storm of improbable
and distorted hallucinations that emanated from his real life. He
was standing there in her foyer, surrounded by a spectral play
of his injuries and failures that was as plastic and mobile and
colorful and ridiculous as the kind of light show that had accom-
panied, in its day, the Hendrix music that she had played for the
general.

She had no music playing now, and this light show was not
funny. The man's mother unkissed and the coach unanswered and

the father unapproached were there, in a swirl, and the impossibly beautiful woman was there, and she was crying, and she was crying for something the man had done or said to her. The man was aroused, and he looked at her—Mrs. Hollingsworth—with a piercing hunger that was at once honest and direct and simple and also hopelessly fraught with reservations and riders and provisos just beneath the surface of his leering desire. It was an irresistibly messy kind of desire. It promised as much pain as balm. He looked like the kind of cat who would bite you on the neck to hold you down and spend days kissing the wound.

Was he a man who wanted but did not need her? Since she stood in a convenient relationship to getting the truth from this kind of man, Mrs. Hollingsworth asked him, "Do you want me?"

To this he said, clear-eyed and broad of shoulder because of the grain sacks, and looking strangely elegant in the cheap shirt, "Yes."

"Do you need me?"

"Need?"

They regarded each other a long time. The man looked at the floor. They heard a sound at the door and the man opened it and the lemon dog came into the house. It began snuffling the baseboards, raptly, undistracted. Every couple of increments forward the dog made a kind of cough, as if clearing its system, like a wine taster between tastes, and then resumed its eager inhalation of her house. It worked one of the boards until out of their sight.

"That's a good dog," the man said. "I had a life in which I would have needed you, once. It was not an honest life. I died. I have a new life. In it I want you, but it would be dishonest of me

158

to need you. If I were to get succor from you, I would not be able to return it properly—I would only take. Then I would repudiate your succor and accuse you of giving it to me. The form of this accusation would be intractable, but that is its substance. You would have, in giving me succor which I could not return, exposed me to be a nonreciprocator of love, and I would have to hate you for this. This hate also would take intractable forms. One of the commoner intractable forms would be a declaration that I wanted yet *another* woman to do this to. I would tell you this to hurt you, and then hurt the new woman the same way. You do not want me to need you. You want me to want you."

This was of course suspiciously convenient-looking to Mrs. Hollingsworth, given her own ruminations concerning men who wanted and needed. But it was also complicated enough that she was not sure she had generated it all. It had an integrity that was stronger than her own formulation would have been, she thought.

She approached the man and put her finger inside the hopeless shirt she had cruelly given him. It seemed a fit emblem of this new life he said he had, though. Previously the shirt would have been a nice powder-blue Brooks Brothers oxford cloth. "What I want," she said, "is for you to take a bath with me."

The lemon dog was working a spot on the living room carpet. It could not advance because it had to do the system-clearing cough at every sniff. It stood in its tracks, snuffling up and discarding invisible olfactory trash. "Too much weirdness in that carpet for him to know anything at all," the man said. "He's got the instinct to give up. He'll move on. I must too." Mrs. Hollings-

worth did not like her man speaking this overtly—she was better than that, she thought, and he was. Still, he said it. She was
going to have to get used to the idea of taking a man for what he
was despite her cartoon of him. She had heard of Michelangelo's
cartoon on the Sistine Chapel ceiling, cut into the plaster, lines
that he had had the genius to ignore once up there on his back
with the truer paintbrush in his hand.

In the scalding tub—the man shied from the water, and whim-
pered and fretted getting in, almost asymptotically, and remarked
that he needed to be sterilized anyway—she laid the man back
against her and held him in her arms. She calmed his eyes by
pressing her hot hands over his eyelids, and she held his breasts,
and her own were trapped against his back in an exhilarating
press of steam and heat, making them tender and alive. She
pushed the man forward and checked them to see if they had
turned into huge wontons, which is what they felt like. His broad
back was gorgeous in that position, and she took a good coarse
washcloth and good glycerine soap to him. She washed him as if,
it occurred to her, they were in the nineteenth century, or whatever century it was or centuries it was that people sat in tubs
and other people poured great gouts of hot water on them and
washed them. How had that disappeared? Maybe that disappear-
ance was the beginning of the hell-in-a-handcart ride the human
world seemed set on. The man leaned forward and accepted this
succor from her without protest.

He began to speak. He spoke at great length, and nothing he
said was intelligible to the ear. Yet she understood everything

he said. It was a modification of the curious phenomenon that Ray Oswald had observed in the Forrest film during the dinner party. It was talk that sounded like talk but was not talk, yet in the present case was understandable to an organ other than the ear and the brain. While he talked, the lemon dog came into the bathroom and stopped its snuffling and sat and regarded the man with its head held atilt as if it understood everything. Mrs. Hollingsworth realized she was listening in the same way.

She realized too she was not capable of reporting what the man was saying, any more than the dog was. But the man was speaking the truth of his life, and to her. It was of the pain of his life, and his smallness, and his failures, and it was offered to her not as something she would need to assume the burden of and help him with, any more than the dog would be asked to help him with it. It was being put into the air more or less as clothes are put into the air before lovers unite. He was taking his clothes off for her. Hers, she felt, were off. She realized that in this respect she was not unlike the dog. This was perhaps what was spectacularly lovable about dogs: their clothes were off at all times, and they did not even know it. People wanted to be that way.

She and the dog listened to the man go on. The room was filled with agreeable steam and the music of this confession that was so complicated, like the carpet the dog could not analyze, that you could only love it and go with it and hum along and kiss the ear of the man singing it, who was singing it not because he needed her to hear it but because he wanted her to hear it, and she did not want to hear it, but she needed to.

She began to see along with the man, to comprehend, as it were, because she could not apprehend what he was saying in the ramble of language that was not talk. The man was seeing that his father who had taken him out of football had also sold his shotgun rather than give it to him, a boy of thirteen who could have used a shotgun. So the disappointment the boy had given the father came before that. The mother was somehow approving of this, the not football and the not gun. The father was known to fight and the mother was also approving that the boy would not be known to fight, though she approved of the father's violence. Had the father had the boy taken from him by the mother? What were the mother's nonfootball nongun nonviolent plans and hopes for her boy, then? Plans so fond that she denied the plans the father had naturally had, in the absence of which the boy would grow up to be afraid of thick-shouldered high school boys because he had not been allowed to be one. And in the absence of which the boy would grow to look distrustfully upon the women who purported to give him succor—what were they really up to? Were they not like his mother? Did they have plans for you that were defined primarily by their not being someone else's plans for you, that alone their virtue?

Facing a woman who meant him well, the boy had become a man in a hollow of doubt. He had kissed his father at the funeral but not his mother. Because of his mother he had not assaulted the man in the funeral home who had insulted them. His father would have assaulted the man, in the parlor or on the very embalming table had the struggle improbably moved from one room to the next. Yet the man who had been the boy whose father would not give him a shotgun or let him play football or teach him to fight or even to gamble at cards could only bluster and threaten and walk out into the blinding sun and see a vision of Forrest riding a horse through sunny hill and dale of grave upon grave.

The lessons he would learn in life would come from hired hands who bore him malice and aimed weapons at him and high school boys who beat him, not from his father. His women would be not sufficiently not his mother. The most honest way he would come to regard them was with the piercing open hunger for them with which he had looked at Mrs. Hollingsworth when he came in her door.

Confused and afraid of life, he would resort to honesty, a fool's tool that would dig a grave more quickly than undiluted corruption. And he lay in Mrs. Hollingsworth's arms in a tub of boiling water, saying all this without knowing what he was saying, but trying. She listened to every word that was not a word and thought him to be taking sustenance from her, from her surreal meal, from her having no plans for him that were not precisely and ineluctably and unpredictably her own.

INTRUDERS IN THE FOG

———◁◦▷———

WHILE THE MAN CARRIED ON with the song of his essential self, articulate in its inarticulateness, important in its triviality, the man and the woman and the dog heard a noise outside the bathroom door. A voice whispered, "She's in here." The woman knew immediately it was the Tupperware daughter she had asked out of the house. She knew she was talking to her father, and that she had dragged him home from his office day on grounds that she, Mrs. Hollingsworth, had lost her mind. She knew that they could not have heard the man mumbling on about himself but that they could have heard her mumbling along with him, completing his wordless squirreled syntax in the not language he was necessarily using. If they opened the door they would not see the man or the dog, only her in her thinning hirsuteness and pink flesh being a boiled human egg in the middle of the live-long day.

The daughter would have also told the husband about the crazy list-making, but she believed the husband to know about it already. She had seen him looking at it once or twice in the drawer where she kept it in the kitchen. He had closed the drawer and asked where the matches were, or the whatever he could think to ask about instead of asking her about the altogether strange thing in the drawer. He had had a queer look on his face that she had not seen there in a long time. It was a smile, an oblique look of impish bemusement. She realized as she lay there expecting to have to cover herself against their door-ramming rescue of her that the look was the same one she had seen on Forrest's face after he said "What is that shit?" referring to the Hendrix music. With them hovering outside the door there was no time to give this revelation justice: had she put her husband's expression on Forrest? If she had, there was more to her husband than she had thought. This was not surprising, because it seemed to her that she had not thought of him *at all* for about fifty years. And now he was a sanity detective hunched over with his ear to the bathroom door behind which she, whom for all she knew he had not thought of for fifty years, lay like a mad steamed dumpling. Nothing this delightful had arranged itself in her real life in a long, long time.

She braced for the invasion, wondering if they might not turn up the volume on NPR to a deafening level to cover the uncivil sounds of shouldering the door. You could be known to hang yourself in your carport in this neighborhood with a measure of dignity, but the breaking down of a door would not do. A woman down the street, it was alleged, had actually chopped apart the hollow-core door to her son's bedroom with an ax to prevent his masturbating. The boy in question was thereafter regarded with small gratuitous kindnesses in the neighborhood, while the mother was shied from in the grocery store. Men in particular kept a cart between themselves and her. Thinking of all this now, Mrs. Hollingsworth realized that the invasion was not forthcoming. The bulk of the bourgeoisie was no longer holding its breath up against the hollow-core door preventing her rescue. She was hearing her husband's voice.

From the sound of it, and some muted noises coming from her daughter, she judged her husband to be sitting where Turner had sat during the dinner party, at the head of the dining table. Her daughter was not where Jane had been but where Oswald had been, at a polite and reserved remove down the table. Oswald, for all his coarseness, and the haircut, had had a fine sense of propriety. "I'd say," her husband was saying, "she is taking a bath."

"Dayad," her daughter said, as condescendingly as a teenager, "how can you—"

"And I'd say what she has written is, you are right, not a grocery list. And to your notion that she has lost her mind, I'd say that I hope you are right."

One of the muted noises escaped her daughter at this. "You *do*?"

"I do."

This was so congruent to Mrs. Hollingsworth's way of thinking during all these days of making her list that she thought perhaps she *had* lost her mind. It was one thing to have Forrest speak the way you wanted him to, for you, or her wounded man with his not need and his want, but quite another to have your husband up and vote right along with you, without the least prompt. She realized that she had loaded in the breach of her mouth something to fire at them had they broken in the door, to protect herself along with the ridiculous gesture of trying to cover herself. She had been about to shout at them, "I'm an *artist!*" With the relief now of what she was hearing her husband say, and realizing she had had this bullet verily on her tongue, she started laughing, and she knew they could hear her. She could imagine her husband gesturing in the air toward her as she laughed, as if to say to the daughter, "See? She is happy. I am right."

But he was saying something much more improbable than that. "Your mother is tired, honey. I am tired. Or I was. Today I am not. I am retired today."

"What?" the daughter said, in a tone of shock and wonder that was extremely gratifying. Mrs. Hollingsworth loved her husband at this moment. She thought it a lie designed to take pressure off her in the daughter's eyes, and to shock the daughter. But she did not believe her husband to be as malicious with respect to the children as she had become. And indeed he was not, for it appeared instantly that he was not lying.

He told the daughter that he was retired and that he and her mother had enough money to live on and that they were liquidating everything and hitting the trail. "I don't know," he said, "if we will take taxis or get a dope van."

"Where are you going?" The tone was now accusing. How had this smooth pea come out of her wrinkled self?

"I don't know that either. We might actually sit right here, but we are going somewhere else nonetheless even if we do not move an inch." Mrs. Hollingsworth almost heard this as "a inch," as if Oswald had said it. Had she put her husband in Oswald too? There was something aggressive in her husband's voice. It was a good voice, a voice he used professionally as a judge, and he could use it well. He could scare a man into straightening up, a jury into nullifying all notion of nullifying itself. He was cranking it up in the living room on his own daughter. He was a quietly desperate man himself, Mrs. Hollingsworth realized. That she might be insane and he desperate gave her a thrill.

Her husband was now carrying on almost like the man in the tub, but with consummate articulation and elocution, bench-grade. Strangely, she could understand what he was saying much less well than she had understood the man in the tub with her, but she could hear that it was the same kind of song, if it was not the same song. The particulars were now daily and daylight ones, for the daughter's benefit. Life was too short to be afraid of it all your life, he was saying, but like this: "There is no dignity in the Volvo. Would you like one?" Ho! He said that! Even odder noises were coming out of the daughter. "No, no, honey. Not give it to you, but Blue Book value," and some huffing purse-sweeping outrage and the door closed and the daughter was gone.

A silence caught the house. It was the ticking of the middling day of the settling suburban house that drove her mad. But there was this new presence in it with her. It sat back at the table. It sighed and, she could see it well, folded its hands in calm regard. It brushed its good haircut back from its temples and looked modestly unkempt and drowsily wild. It was tired. It was retired.

It was going to get up in a minute or two and come get in the tub with her. This development was positively luminescent in its improbability, in its corniness, in its fairy-tale dynamic and melodrama. She had written her husband back into her life, her life back into itself; they maybe had one where before they had not. That this had happened was not, she thought—adjusting some heat into the tub via a hose that would make no sound, so that she could hear her husband move toward her—to be looked hard in the mouth. It was to be ridden. If anything happened, they were to fight or run, according to whether it was time to fight or run. Mrs. Hollingsworth knew all about it.

Her husband's cologne came through the door before him. It was of course the same cologne Forrest had worn and that she had dabbed on many times herself. He got in the tub in the same position as the wounded man. He did not say a word.

His legs were out in front of them, like something on exhibit, straight and narrow and suit-pale. He shimmied them, setting up a small standing wave of ripples in the tub, and stopped and held his legs still. "I wonder if I can still run," he said.

Mrs. Hollingsworth put her whole tongue in his ear, like a teenager. "If I can still do that," she said, "you can still run. Did you really retire?"

"I am as retired as a dog ready for another dog to lie on top of him."

Startled, Mrs. Hollingsworth said, "Hey! General Forrest said that!"

Her husband said, "I know General Forrest said that. Anybody went to Nathan Bedford Forrest High School knows that."

"Anybody went" was Ray Oswald. Dogs under dogs was Forrest. The whole thing had been her husband, her apprehensions of fifty or a hundred too-familiar years with her husband, whom she had found again by making him a list, a list of her husband, a meal at last for him. And the man she had taken out of powder-blue oxford cloth and put in red plaid was her husband, wounded and tired on pin legs in her tub.

The best things in the universe are the out-of-mind and the invisible, those sunny caves of ice you forget when you wake up —as Coleridge put it before his hybridity was adjudicated. Mrs. Hollingsworth distrusted the fairy-taleness of all this, but not enough to not believe it. She and her husband had emerged from stupefaction, and she was not going to gainsay it. They were going to get on the horse of this new life, real or not, and ride. They were going to tear the very air with determination to win. They were not going to inspect the cause or weigh their slim chances. "Come in the bedroom, love," she said to her retired skinny-legged husband. "You be canvas and I'll be silk. I'll be a thimble, you be silver. I'll melt you into the ground. There is no operator's manual for my gizmo."

Her husband stood up and got himself a towel and headed for the bedroom. He had nothing on but that impish look, and he said not a word, a retired judge.

ABOUT THE AUTHOR

Padgett Powell is the author of six novels, including *The Interrogative Mood* and *You & Me.* His novel *Edisto* was a finalist for the National Book Award. His writing has appeared in the *New Yorker, Harper's Magazine, Little Star,* and the *Paris Review,* and he is the recipient of the Rome Fellowship in Literature from the American Academy of Arts and Letters, as well as the Whiting Writers' Award. He lives in Gainesville, Florida, where he teaches writing at MFA@FLA, the writing program of the University of Florida.

EBOOKS BY PADGETT POWELL

FROM OPEN ROAD MEDIA

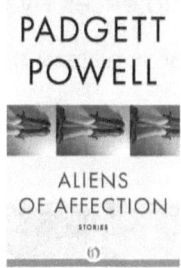

Available wherever ebooks are sold